The Seraph En

by

I.O. Adler

Old Chrome Book One

CW00377284

Chapter One

There were three things Miles Kim didn't like about the bandits who had stopped the atomic grav train bound for Seraph.

First, one of the robbers, a rangy puke wearing a tattered duster and a paisley bandana around his mouth, had punched the porter, who had unlocked the passenger car to let the two men in. The porter's nose gushed blood as he cowered with the riders at the frontmost seats.

Second, both the little girls across from Miles who had been crying and fussing during the first half of their five-hour journey but had been finally distracted by their dad playing travel bingo and singing Tagalog lullabies were crying again. Their parents had them huddled and were attempting to calm them down.

And third, Miles was going to miss his appointment with the man who was scheduled to kill him.

The lanky bandit who had done the punching shoved his partner forward. The second robber was shorter, smaller, and, now that Miles glimpsed his face, looked about twelve years old. The kid held a burner in one hand and a pillowcase in the other.

"Give everything in your pockets to him," the lanky bandit shouted. There was an electronic buzz to his voice. An augmentation? "Anyone who hesitates gets a hole in the head."

Most of the passengers sat stunned, some gasped, and the man sitting next to Miles began to mewl softly. The family across from Miles shrank as if they hoped to disappear altogether. But not everyone was cowed, and this worried Miles.

On a seat right behind the family of four was a woman wearing a plum waistcoat and a matching petite riding hat. She had been staring at Miles throughout the ride, which wasn't unusual, but she hadn't looked away when he caught her. Instead she had given him a bemused smile. She spent most of the trip writing on her device, using a purple fingernail as a stylus.

And at the back of the passenger car was a marshal transporting a prisoner. Miles had spotted them instantly when boarding, the marshal trying to keep low key with his prisoner's manacles concealed beneath a coat. But there was no hiding the fist-sized weapon on the marshal's hip or the badge clipped to his belt. The prisoner got cuffed every time he tried to strike up a conversation with anyone.

As Miles glanced back between the seats, the marshal adjusted himself and his weapon rig.

Eyes forward again, Miles stifled a curse.

Of all the ways a bandit might relieve the travelers on board the Seraph Express of their pocket credits, jumping on board a train waving a burner about while shouting "this is a stickup" was easily the worst. And the last thing he needed was to be caught in a firefight with a trigger-happy hero.

The kid went from passenger to passenger with his gun pointing unsteadily. His voice held a prepubescent pitch when he screeched, "Hand it over!" He made it to the family across the aisle. The mother dropped in what they had without comment.

Miles scooched down in his chair, keeping his head bowed so his black round-rim hat would cover most of his face. The young bandit's feet were visible as he continued past, collecting devices, wallets, and jewelry. The kid had his back to Miles and was finishing with the opposite side of the car, robbing the woman with the purple hat and then a group of four older women who gave up their belongings with little more than reproachful glares.

Someone outside was shouting. Yellow sands swirled beyond the window, but whoever was out there wasn't visible. Because the track and train were elevated, Miles would have to crane his neck to see, and he wanted nothing upsetting the robbers.

Miles stole another glance back as the kid made it to the marshal. The kid was hurrying now. He barely paused as the marshal dropped a wallet and device into the proffered loot bag without comment. The kid skipped the prisoner and a few of the other passengers.

The marshal's steel-eyed glare followed, which the kid missed as he approached the seats directly behind Miles.

Meanwhile, the gangly robber at the front of the car had vanished outside.

Amateurs.

What did amaze Miles was the fact the robbers had stopped the train. The Insight module installed in his head gave the specifics of the train's nuclear engine, the weight of the cars, and how fast they had been going. A bullet train leaves River City via Devil's Bridge on its way to Seraph going 600 kph. How long will it take to reach your destination if a rangy puke and a boy not old enough to shave hit the brakes somewhere past the halfway point?

"Enough with the infodump, Insight," he muttered.

With a hard double blink, the barrage of data vanished. The train was big, had been cruising faster than anything most of these new generation planet-born kids had seen, and it wouldn't stop for anything. Passengers couldn't leave unless they busted out a tamper-proof window and jumped.

Yet here they were, going 0 kph at a few minutes to noon and over an hour from their destination.

The mewling man next to him surrendered his valuables.

"Let me see your hands, old timer," the kid said.

Miles raised them. Wouldn't look up.

"Device? Wallet? Come on, come on, come on!"

The kid sounded even younger than before. Was he reciting lines from a serial? Moving as slow as he could, Miles dipped a hand into his suit coat and removed a pocketbook which contained his credit chips. The bandit wiggled the pillowcase so Miles could drop it in.

"What about your mobile device?" the young bandit asked. *"Come on!"*

"I don't carry one."

The kid reached over the mewling man, who let out a fresh squeak, and patted Miles down. He held the gun awkwardly and it would have been an easy grab. As advertised, the young bandit found nothing worth taking, and he left alone the paper card and envelope Miles kept in his inside suit pocket.

Miles caught a whiff of booze.

The bandit's hand gripping the burner looked soft and the fingernails trimmed. But what Miles thought was a glove on the kid's bag hand turned out to be a synthetic limb. Graphene-steel composite, tough, high density, but without fake skin, so the implant wasn't high end.

With the gun, the kid tapped the lapel of Miles' black suit. "You look like you're dressed up for a funeral."

"Maybe I am."

It was the first good look Miles had of the kid's face. Barely a hint of stubble on his chin. Sunburned cheeks.

The kid flipped Miles' hat off and gasped.

Despite the burner pointing at him, Miles tried not to grin. It was a reaction he was used to. Was it the metal plates visible beneath the grafts of fake skin? The deactivated ports behind his jawline where an old school input cable could be plugged? Or the white right eye which contrasted with his hazel left eye? An experienced observer would know an ocular range finder and targeting system with no cosmetic pretensions when they saw one. Everything attached to his head was old, the type of thing the meat-and-metal hacks slapped on the soldiers to get them back into the thick of things. While Meridian had its share of cyborgs, there weren't many like Miles Kim walking around these days.

"They don't make 'em as pretty as me anymore," Miles said to the kid.

The burner kept waving near his face. The kid almost fumbled his weapon as he adjusted the bag and cinched it beneath an arm. Miles could have snatched it away, but the kid had a finger on the trigger. And the sooner the kid left, the sooner they could get underway.

The Insight module's facts began rolling in once more, with an uninvited feed in Miles' field of vision displaying the characteristics of the robber's burner: single or burst laser-plasma weapon, capable of ten shots at full power before a battery swap, ergonomic handle, possible encoding restriction feature, snap beam, with pricing options not available as his module wasn't connected to the net.

"You got my money. You're doing great. Now watch that laser," Miles said.

"You're...you're..."

"Nobody. And that hand doesn't look like it fits you. Are we done here, kid? You're ahead of the game with that sack of loot. Time for you to go."

"Don't call me kid."

"I don't want to call you anything. I want you to take your winnings and get off this train so we can get going. Sound good?"

The kid still stared.

The darker corners of Meridian had markets for old tech. Maybe the kid wasn't in shock but was sizing up a bigger score than a pillowcase full of credit chips and mobile phones. As the bandit's graphene hand was either a poor fit from a cut-rate surgeon or stolen off someone who no longer needed it, such a robbery might still be on the table.

Whoever was shouting outside shouted again, louder this time, and there were multiple voices. The young bandit glanced over his shoulder towards the door.

The lanky robber appeared at the front of the car. "Hurry up!"

The kid scurried up the aisle. Miles bent down to pick up his hat when the marshal sprang to his feet and produced his palm-sized hand cannon. As the marshal strode past, he raised the weapon.

Without thinking, Miles pushed past the mewling man and grabbed the marshal, turning the gun towards the ceiling. It fired. The shattering boom sent a shockwave through the train car and hurt Miles' ears and teeth. Plastic debris rained down on them.

"Get off me!" the marshal barked.

"They're not alone, you idiot."

As if punctuating the comment, a window exploded. Another popped, then a burning hole appeared in the ceiling. Anyone who hadn't ducked already hit the floor as more incoming burner fire battered the car. The marshal and Miles kept their heads down.

At the front of the car, the two bandits were gone.

"I had him," the marshal said.

"He was just the bag boy. And if you had blasted him, they might be doing more than just covering their getaway."

The incoming fire stopped. Miles crawled forward to the open door and peered out through an open hatch to the outside. The desert lay beyond. A curtain of dust rose, which didn't conceal some dozen riders on horseback and motorbike who raced away from the train.

They joined a second group, which appeared to be coming from the engine at the front. At least seventeen in the gang, by Miles' count.

The woman with the purple hat crouched next to him. "Is it safe?"

Miles got up and dusted off his hat. "They're leaving. No one lost anything they can't replace." He went to the porter with the bloody nose. "Check and see if anyone's hurt in the rest of the cars. And then find out how long it's going to take to get this train moving."

The porter nodded and went to a wall panel. "Power's out, and I can't open the doors to the other car."

"Then we go outside and head to the front."

The marshal pushed Miles against the bulkhead. "You're not going any-where."

Miles tried to dislodge the man, but the marshal was larger and proved stronger.

He nudged Miles' ribs with the hand cannon. "You're with them, aren't you? That's why you stopped me."

"What are you talking about?"

The passenger car fell into a hush. They had everyone's undivided attention.

The marshal sneered. "Just pointing out the obvious. You're one of those good-for-nothing Metal Heads."

Chapter Two

The marshal kept a hand gripping the back of Miles' coat. The big man blinked hard as his brow glistened with sweat. The hand cannon hadn't moved from Miles' side.

Miles did his best to not flinch. "If you could please not crease the suit."

"I'm going to get cuffs off my belt. You're going to put them on."

"If that'll calm you down, then fine. You're in charge."

The marshal released the coat and took a step back. Began fumbling with something under his coat. The barrel of the hand cannon bobbed and weaved. Finally, he produced a set of handcuffs.

The woman with the fancy purple hat stood demurely by with grave concern on her face. "Gentlemen, if I may be so bold? There are more pressing issues at hand. We're stopped in the middle of the desert. The ones who actually robbed us are getting away."

"One of their number isn't," the marshal said.

She snatched the cuffs. "Don't be foolish. Our friend here just stopped you from making an unpleasant situation worse. Now can we see what the condition of the train is?"

"I'm placing him under arrest."

"Correct me if I'm wrong, marshal, but we're not in Seraph city territory yet. And seeing as how we're past Devil's Bridge, we're not in Meridian territory either. This is a Herron-Cauley train on a Herron-Cauley track. Private property—"

"Look, missy, why don't you sit back down and let the professionals handle this? We got a lot of scared passengers here—"

"And Mr. Kim is one of them."

Miles had kept silent during the exchange but the woman knowing his name made him study her face. The Insight module measured her specific dimensions, ear shape, eye, skin, and hair color, but came up blank. No surprise. There hadn't been a software update since Miles jailbroke the hardware, and he had kept it offline since then.

"Who are you?" he asked the woman.

"Someone who wants to make it to Seraph in a timely manner." She fished a thin device from a waistcoat pocket and tapped the screen before showing it to the marshal.

"Great," the marshal said scornfully. "A lawyer."

"Dawn Moriti, attorney-at-law in Meridian, and registered counsel in Seraph. Both recognize Herron-Cauley sovereignty over its trains and tracks. Which means you're here as our guest, Marshal Barma."

"Well, this *guest* is telling you that your train was just robbed. The criminals stole our wallets and phones and threatened us, and here you are wasting my time."

"You'll be compensated for your lost property. In fact, everyone here will be."

"I saw you hand your device over," Miles said.

Dawn tried to contain a smile. "How observant. Our little bandit missed this one."

The marshal put the cuffs away. He gave Miles a final disapproving look before heading towards the front of the car and the exit. "Well then, Dawn Moriti, you keep an eye on him. I'm going outside to check if they're gone."

"What about your prisoner?" Miles asked.

"Him? He'll stay in his seat if he knows what's good for him."

As the marshal stepped out, Miles moved to follow.

"And where are you going?" Dawn said. "We should stay here."

"The marshal's right; we need to know if those guys left. And then there's the matter of your train."

She protested as he stepped through the open hatch and out into the desert. The hot air hit his face like a stuffy blanket. He adjusted his hat to keep the sunlight out of his eyes. The marshal had climbed down to the concrete rail bed and was surveying the horizon. Miles joined him.

"Get back up on the train," the marshal said.

With his eye implant, Miles confirmed that there wasn't anyone on the port side of the train in sight, but a low ridge and a drop-off a hundred meters distant might conceal a company of fresh bad guys. The haze of the departing gang continued to linger. The air carried a singed plastic smell, no doubt from the burner holes the gang had put into the train.

Up ahead, passengers were climbing down from the other train cars. The various groups were milling about as if they were lost or had detrained on an alien world. One of the forward cars had smoke trickling from its window.

"You called them Metal Heads?" Miles asked.

The marshal gave him a disdainful look. "I saw you adjust your window just before they hit us."

"What, pulling the shade? You think they had a spotter which could see us as we were going half the speed of sound?"

.47 the speed of sound, atmospheric factors not taken into account.

Shut up, Insight.

"It's none of your business what I think. Don't lurk behind me. And if you so much as look at me funny, I don't care what any lawyer says, I'm putting a hole in your shiny head."

"So long as we know where we stand with each other."

Miles skidded down the embankment to the hardpan and headed towards the front of the train. The smoke poured from one of the windowless cars. Cargo, no doubt, as it was behind the engine sections. The marshal lumbered after him. Sweat dripped from his face.

"I don't like you out here," the marshal said.

"If my fellow Metal Heads had a sniper, they'd have shot you by now."

The marshal checked the landscape again.

They approached the first milling group. A fidgety woman in a plaid business suit stepped forward and was shielding her eyes with a pamphlet.

"Oh, thank goodness. Lawmen. Those criminals robbed us."

"I'm Marshal Barma. And this is no lawman."

"Anyone hurt?" Miles asked.

The woman squinted as if trying to make out Miles' face. "No, I don't believe so. They blasted open the luggage car and were rummaging through it. They took a case out. My furniture is back there. My fabricator. My oven. Will you please check if they were damaged?"

Miles walked past her. The breach in the freight car appeared as if the side hatch had been blown with explosives. The remaining steel was curled like a peeled orange skin. Someone had been in a hurry or lacked the skill to hack the electronic door locks. He grabbed the handrail and pulled himself up to the car. The hatch between train cars remained sealed and intact. A red light was blinking. Either a power outage or other alert, but the car wouldn't let him in through the hatch, and an input screen remained blank when he touched it.

Getting to the breach required climbing along the outside of the train.

"Anyone in there?" Miles said. "I'm here to help."

Both the marshal and the lawyer ascended the railbed and were standing beneath him.

"There were no security personnel on the manifest," Dawn said.

"Good thing." He peered into the car's interior. It was dark and smoke lingered. The closest object on the floor appeared to be a rosewood headboard with hand-carved scrollwork. Half of it was splintered. The shattered remains of an armoire lay just beyond it.

So much for the furniture.

Contrary to the manifest, a guard lay sprawled among the debris. Had a pulse, still breathing. Miles relieved him of a burner and kept the weapon in hand. Late model, virtual scope, able to fire twenty shots as fast as you can pull the trigger. Better than anything the bandits carried, or that the Meridian military had these years.

Of the locked compartments along each wall, most, if not all, appeared intact. Here was where the passengers could stow any belongings they didn't want on them during their transit. But if the bandits had the explosives to get on board, why hadn't they gone after more?

Perhaps they weren't amateurs. But no quick-response law enforcement would arrive here as they would in River City and other parts of Meridian. So why the big hurry? What had they taken?

It reminded Miles of an ancient proverb his wife had quoted time and time again when encouraging him to mind his own business: "Not my circus, not my monkeys."

Time to get the train moving. Let Marshal Barma and the Herron-Cauley people figure it out. But the marshal had walked off.

"We need a medic for the guard," Miles told Dawn. "He's breathing."

Dawn passed along the message as more of the passengers emerged from the train and stood outside the freight car. A couple of men climbed on board and began providing first aid to the guard. A porter brought a stretcher.

Miles swung down from the car and got out of the way. "No security? Then who is that?"

"They must have added a guard last minute," Dawn said. "An oversight."

"What's the word on the engine?"

Dawn had her device out but appeared to be having trouble. "The train's network is down."

The marshal was hurrying in their direction from the front of the train. His face was flush. "The engineers are working on it. Something jacked the electrical system." Then he pointed at Miles. "Why is he armed?"

"That's what you're worried about, Mr. Barma?" Dawn asked.

Miles had the burner at his side. With one quick motion, he spun the barrel and handed the weapon grip-first to the marshal. The marshal took it without comment.

The men in the freight car had the unconscious guard on the stretcher and were strapping him down. The woman in the plaid suit appeared eager for someone to help her climb up.

Dawn was fanning herself while trying to keep the sun off her face. "Well, this has been an exciting day. Mr. Kim, what say we retire back to our seats and let the marshal handle this. I'm sure we'll be underway soon."

While Miles wasn't optimistic about the train keeping its schedule, he knew there was no point in interfering with the engineers who he hoped knew what they were doing. And it was hot. The marshal appeared more than willing to supervise the situation.

Yet something about the incident bothered him. He wanted to know more about these Metal Heads. If they were nothing but a hard-scrabble desert gang of thieves with a few off-market implants, then how had they robbed a train run by one of the leading Meridian corporations? This hadn't been a brute force attack but a surgical strike. The two robbers he had seen were acting separately from the main heist, which had broken into the freight car. That explained why they appeared to be playing things loose.

Poor leadership, he decided. Something he had been long accustomed to after decades in the Meridian military. Things got sloppy further down the organizational ladder when there were no good junior officers and noncoms to keep the grunts in line.

Mystery solved. He followed Dawn towards the back of the train. But something in the distance caught his eye. He once again scanned the line of desert.

Motion, a murmur in the rising lines of heat. It appeared smaller than man-sized. A dog? As he focused with his eye module, he caught a flash of red.

Laser.

"Get down!"

He shoved Dawn to the ground and ran past her. Most laser weapons had a delay for any kind of aimed shot. He wasn't waiting to see who the target was as he raced for the freight car.

"Hit the ground!"

The marshal and the men helping the fallen guard on the stretcher froze in place. A flash. A man went to the ground, screaming and clutching the charred stump of his wrist. Miles grabbed the marshal and got him down as a second passenger dropped, a round singe mark marring his forehead.

The others scattered, the injured freight car guard and stretcher tumbling as men and women began diving down the embankment or hurtling themselves towards the track buttresses. More impacts followed, the freight car peppered by a barrage of flashes. Holes melted in the smooth hull. A rock in front of Miles exploded, sending fragments spraying against his face.

He pulled the marshal with him and grabbed one end of the stretcher. Together, they hauled the injured guard to cover beneath the train.

The incoming fire continued, zapping the ground and train above as Miles and the marshal kept their heads down. After what felt like minutes but Insight confirmed was only ten seconds, the burner fire ceased.

Miles peered up from the concrete and focused on the location where he had spotted the shooter. Too small for a bandit, even the kid. So what was out there? Why snipe the passengers after the gang had made a clean getaway?

The dark lump remained in place. The laser no longer flashed.

"Give me the guard's burner," Miles whispered.

"Like hell."

"I see him." It. But this wasn't time for semantics. "If you think you can get him from here, be my guest."

Dawn was elbow-crawling her way beneath the train. A sheen of gray dust covered her face, her hat was missing, and her dark hair hung in a tumbling tangle. "Give him the laser, marshal."

Was the marshal's face turning a deeper shade of red? He handed the guard's weapon over. Miles sighted in. His eyepiece told him everything he needed to know. And the burner? A perfect weapon in his hands. Unlike a slug thrower, he didn't have to account for drop, windage, or air resistance. He braced himself on the buttress. Hesitated.

The marshal spat grit from his mouth, all the while keeping his head to the concrete. "You see them? Then what are you waiting for?"

Miles' target remained highlighted in red. But new shapes appeared. First two, then six, and then fourteen, all lined up along the sandy ridge. They crept like spiders emerging from the ground. Once they took their position, they grew perfectly still.

Waiting.

And as if by an unseen command, all of them switched on lasers, which aimed straight at the train.

Chapter Three

"Take cover!"

Miles hugged the buttress as burner fire once again sizzled into the train. Passengers began crawling down the opposite side of the track. Others still on board were jumping, some falling, and others diving, heedless of injuries as the train had not deployed ladders or any of its emergency evacuation slides.

The laser fire continued indiscriminately, the shooters appearing content to fire wildly at the train. Each shot let out a soft hiss and pop. The burning smell intensified, and something on the train above them was on fire, judging by a growing bank of white smoke descending around them.

A few passengers remained exposed on the ground beneath the port side of the train. Easy targets, yet they hadn't been shot down. Too many voices were screaming and calling for help.

Miles lined up on the first spider, the target lock reconfirming his selection. The burner trigger felt light as he eased his finger into the finger guard.

Fired. The *hum-fizz* was soft and anticlimactic, but the spider flipped over and vanished behind the ridgeline. Miles sighted on the next spider, already pre-selected by his eye. Fired. Next target. Fired again. Miles squeezed off seven more shots, each requiring little more than the slightest pivot as his training and enhancements took over.

But he had no clear shot at the remaining spiders. He crawled forward past the buttress, then incoming laser fire exploded around him, forcing him back behind the slope of the track bed.

Dawn was using him as cover. "You got their attention. Maybe they'll clear out. How many did you hit?"

"Ten, which don't appear to be moving anymore. At least four left."

Exactly four, but Miles didn't want to brag. If there were more beneath the sands or below the horizon, they remained out of sight.

"So, are we past calling for their surrender?" the marshal asked.

"It's not the gang. Whatever's out there is some kind of bot."

"Huh. Probably meant to keep us from chasing the Metal Heads."

Made sense, at least as good as any theory Miles could come up with. But ground crawlers like that weren't cheap. It begged the question of how the gang could muster that kind of equipment loadout. No bag of personal data devices would be worth risking that level of hardware. The unknown was what the gang had stolen from the freight car.

But as long as any of the spiders remained, the train wasn't going anywhere, and the marshal appeared content to let Miles handle it.

A red light on the back of the burner winked. Overheated? But if the newer weapon had an integration feature, it wasn't talking to him, and Insight was no help. He popped the battery out of the grip.

A chunk of concrete exploded near his head. He got down. The remaining bots had him as their target now.

The marshal likewise began trying to become one with the ground. "What's wrong?"

"Error light. Should have ten more shots."

"Give it here."

Miles handed the weapon behind him without rising a centimeter. The marshal only took a moment, turning it off and on again before setting the burner aside.

"There's a crack beneath the barrel. It's busted. Something must have damaged it during the explosion. Lucky you got the shots you did before it got hot."

"What about your handgun?" Dawn asked.

Miles didn't even have to look up. "Not at this range. Doesn't matter what kind of sights you have with that little thing."

The marshal inched forward, his hand cannon in both hands. *KA-KRAK!* The shot sent off a shockwave, the report causing Miles' ears to ring. The marshal fired again, then a third time, but when he squeezed the trigger again, nothing.

"Feel better about yourself?" Miles asked.

"We can't just wait to be shot down," the marshal replied.

"Well, they're not getting any closer. Any more guards? Or other passengers we can find who are packing a weapon?"

Dawn peered at him over her arms. "No other guards unless there were any off duty catching a ride. Ore runs go the other way, not towards Seraph, and not on this line. And no one carries a weapon on our trains. They have to be checked."

All three looked up at the train. The luggage car would have the property lockers. The marshal began reloading, manually inserting four new cartridges into the breach of his pistol. Miles and Dawn crept towards the guard on the stretcher.

Dawn yanked a key card from the guard's, then whispered, "This will get the lockers open. I'll give it to the marshal. It's his job, not yours."

Miles put his hand out. "If there's a burner on board, I'm the one who'll make the shot. Any other way into that freight car?"

She handed over the key card. "Not with the power down, unless you have an engineer's key. The chief's up front in the engine, so that's no good. The manual locks disengage from the inside."

The bots kept firing at regular intervals, an impact every second. All of Miles' instincts told him to crawl to the opposite side of the train and take cover with the rest of the passengers. But if he was listening to his instincts, he wouldn't be in such a hurry to make it to Seraph.

He approached the buttress and the waiting marshal. "You can get your four shots somewhere close to those things?"

The marshal nodded. He held four more cartridges in his hands. "Not all of us have a computer to do our shooting for us. Just do your part. I don't fancy getting a hole burned in my skull by a blasted machine."

"You can also plug an electric tea kettle into my head."

The marshal didn't even crack a grin as he edged into a firing position. "Eight shots and then you're on your own."

"On three. Your count."

"Can't even see 'em," he grumbled. "One...two..."

Miles rolled out from beneath the car as the marshal opened fire, letting off four measured blasts a heartbeat apart. Not enough time. The lasers winked on the ridge. A handrail Miles was about to grab flashed and burst into a flower of sparks. Running now, Miles darted for the opening and dove up, desperately searching for anything to help him climb. Another laser burst seared the air just above him as he clamped a hand onto a pallet jack and pulled himself up, crawling forward and out of sight.

The marshal's cannon was firing again, and no more laser shots came at him, at least for the moment.

At the far side of the car stood the lockers. Miles counted fifty of them, each the size of a shoebox or larger. He began swiping the card, opening one after another, finding most empty and a few with parcels or bundles of personal belongings he couldn't waste any precious seconds to sift through.

New laser holes appeared in the car, letting in pin-sized beams of sunlight.

Miles began throwing the locker items out behind him: small suitcases, sealed and wrapped boxes, bundles of produce and gift baskets, and even a shrink-wrapped package of collared, starched shirts. A weapon rig clunked to the train car floor. The shirts had been sitting on top of a black nylon shoulder holster with a boxy nickel-finish burner tucked inside it.

He pulled the weapon free. Battery held a charge. Five shots. Glowing sights and a tiny laser target flared to life as he gripped it. An electric red etching along the barrel read *Beverly*.

He suppressed a shudder and mentally thanked the weapon's owner, be they Beverly or someone who just named their pistol. He went to the breach and crouched, mentally preparing himself.

Roll out, aim, fire once, take cover. With his elevated position, he felt confident he would spot all the bots, but they'd have a clear line on him, too. As their lasers were powerful enough to penetrate the car, ducking would only decrease his chance of getting hit. He needed a few seconds to get a good scan. His tracking software had accounted for his movements, but if the bots had adjusted their position, he'd waste burner charges.

He grabbed for a piece of luggage. After opening all the zipper pouches, he found a toiletry kit. Razor, creams, toothbrush, mirror.

Bingo.

Mirror in hand, he used the reflection to survey the ridgeline. His hand was trembling. Forced himself to calm down, but knew adrenaline was going to do its thing. Unless he could take a few deep breaths and brace up, hitting the bots with a snapshot was hardly certain, and unlike the guard's weapon, the little burner in his hand felt like a toy.

Where were they?

Found one. A single dark lump. The incoming laser fire had stopped. The lump wasn't moving. He peered out and zoomed in, feeling a prickling sensation running down his neck. There he was, sticking his head up from perfectly suitable cover like a rookie, begging to get shot.

But the other bots were gone. While the landscape could hide any number of the mechanical creatures, he felt they had held nothing back before when forcing the train and the passengers to take cover. Either they were dug in or retreating. And if this last bot was waiting on something, Miles didn't want to hesitate. Sometimes the enemy handed you a mistake on a silver platter. This bot had left itself exposed.

He took aim. Touched the trigger. A fraction of a second later, he had his virtual firing solution.

When he squeezed the trigger, nothing happened. Squeezed again, harder this time, a third time with enough force that he knew the shot would be spoiled.

There in the weapon's grip was an almost invisible recessed square, which he had missed in his haste. A fingerprint authenticator. Beverly wasn't going to fire for anyone but Beverly, or whoever owned her.

He set the pistol aside when motion caught his eye.

A tiny antenna stuck up from the bot's head. A yellow light pulsed, flashing the train as if sending a signal. Not a signal, a laser, and not a weapon. It was targeting the freight car.

Miles looked up. If it weren't for his eye, he would have missed it. There, soaring a kilometer above them, the size of a hawk, and diving, came a drone.

Chapter Four

"Get away from the train! Incoming!"

Miles didn't wait to see if anyone else was following as he dove from the freight car and tumbled, hitting the rocky slope beyond the rail hard and falling head over heels. He sprawled face forward to the base of the rail bed. Covered his head with his arms.

The explosion knocked the breath from his lungs and threw him into the air. He landed hard and curled into a ball as steel, plastic, and rocks rained down around him. The deluge of debris finally ended. Move, his brain kept telling him. But it took all his strength to prove to his body that the ground was down and wasn't going anywhere.

A carpet of choking haze drifted around him. At least the smoke would hinder laser fire. His legs shook as he rose unsteadily. Could barely see the train, but the smoke billowed through a fresh gap between the sections where the freight car used to be. His head felt stuffed with cotton and his mouth tasted of burned sand.

Almost without conscious thought, he trotted forward, stumbling more than once across the uneven ground. In his mental haze, he had a faint idea of direction. The ridge lay ahead of him. If the bots were waiting, he'd be dead. But lying out in the open would have the same result.

Get off the X had been ground into his DNA from the first day of combat training. He heard vague shouts from behind him, but the ringing in his ears obscured everything.

The ridge was higher and steeper than he thought. He clawed and grabbed at the sickly dried roots of some tree which hadn't quite succumbed to the harsh desert or whatever microorganism soup the men on the moon had been dumping down onto the planet to restore it into the semblance of a livable place where man could once again exist without an atmosphere suit. Clumps of alkali clay broke loose as he finished the climb on his hands and feet.

Somewhere along the line he had lost the burner. At least it would have served as a hand weapon. He wasn't sure what he was expecting to do once he made the ridge.

The destroyed spiders lay where they had fallen, like knocked-down targets at a shooting range. Ugly, misshapen, with parts mismatching and having no semblance of uniform design, each spider appeared as if a child had slapped it together out of spare robot parts. Servos, actuators, a small battery power plant, and the damned lasers all sat atop a six-leg chassis. Seven or eight legs on a few of them, he corrected himself as he scanned the wreckage.

The bot with the targeting laser wasn't there, nor did he find any of the remaining spiders he hadn't shot down. He kicked at the remains. None of them had armor. If they did, a single hand burner blast wouldn't have done it. So where had the other bots gone?

With the spindly feet, they left little in the way of marks on the hardpan and rocks. But near where the spider with the targeting laser had stood, multiple tire and hoofprints led away from the scene.

A series of curses erupted from down the slope. The marshal was trying to climb towards him and only succeeded when he crawled on his knees.

"Any...anything?" Marshal Barma gasped.

"The last ones took off."

The marshal stooped to inspect one of the wrecked spiders. "Pretty good shooting, even for a combat model."

"You're talking about me? I wasn't a combat model."

The big man gave a mirthless laugh. "Whatever. At least they're gone."

Miles couldn't miss the marshal keeping him in view. And the hand cannon was back on his gun belt, grip out and ready for a quick draw. Had he kept a few cartridges?

"How many injured?" Miles asked.

"The bot snipers got two. One dead, another hurt, not counting the guard in the baggage car. The lawyer is checking the wreckage. But no one was in the car that blew up. A couple of people have bumps and bruises from jumping out of the train."

"Maybe it's time we check on the engineers. It's hot out and there are a lot of folks standing in the sun."

The marshal let Miles lead the way back to the train.

***

"This engine isn't going anywhere," the train's chief engineer told Miles and the marshal. "The electric system reboots and shuts down every time I try to turn it on. The power plant fail safes won't disengage. It means we go nowhere, and that's assuming the train or the tracks aren't damaged."

The chief engineer was a reed-thin fellow with bushy eyebrows and a sharp nose. There was a plastic quality to his eyes, and he had multiple bulging veins visible on his neck. A spacer, Miles concluded, or at least someone born with a few of the engineered genes which made microgravity survivable over the long term.

He had two assistants working on tablet computers wired to a control panel. The view from the command compartment was surprisingly serene and oblivious to the wreckage to the rear, with the track before them and the wide desert and hills beyond looking like a scene from an Earth recruitment still.

Come back to Earth. Reclaim our home.

The engineer was showing the marshal a screen from his own computer, an electric system diagnostic tool. The marshal nodded along as if he were following the explanation.

"Once home base sees us missing, they'll send the repair crew," the engineer concluded.

Miles paced, peering over the shoulders of the other two techs. One gave him a nervous look, so he headed for the back of the locomotive and climbed outside.

The marshal caught up with him. "Where are you going? I want you to stay in my sights."

"We're doing this again?"

"Seems to me you knocking down a bunch of target dummies doesn't clear you from the suspect list. Either you stay close or I cuff you to a seat. Which will it be?"

"Your pick. But you're not doing much to help get us going. You'd think someone would have reached help by now. Dawn Moriti had her phone. So let's check with her."

Miles could tell by Dawn's expression she had reached no one. Standing in the thin shade beneath their passenger car, she was staring at her device as if it had offended her. "It's like all the towers everywhere are down. Or someone's jamming us. I had the porters check with the other passengers. Everyone who still has their device is experiencing the same thing."

Yet she still tapped at her screen like she was hoping for a new result, as if the situation had resolved itself since her last attempt seconds before.

Miles sat on the lip of the concrete rail bed. "Then we wait on the repair crews to come save us."

Late. He knew he was going to be late, and he would have to reschedule with the surgeon. Would his resolve change? No. It just meant starting from square one in finding the surgeon's middleman in Seraph and hope he had enough funds to smooth over the ruffled feathers. His deposit would be forfeited.

He took out the card from his suit coat pocket. The bland image of sunflowers in a glass vase done in watercolor decorated the front. The inside was blank. What to say?

He had thought about what last message to write his son Dillan, bouncing between an expression of hope for his son's future, a mild admonition to never forget his parents, or an apology. Perhaps one of his wife's—Dillan's mother's—aphorisms? She always had the right expression to place things into perspective. But no, not enough room for any of that, with his handwriting. Yet the white interior felt as vast and unfillable as a canyon he could never hope to cross.

A credit chit would fit just fine within the envelope.

And for that to happen, he needed to meet the surgeon.

He put the card away, then rose and dusted his black suit off. A film of dirt remained on his clothes. It was to be the last thing he wore, soiled now because of the gang of robbers.

"How far away are the repair crews?" Miles asked.

Dawn remained distracted. "That's the thing, there's a substation every hundred klicks. They should have received an automated message the instant the train cut transmission. A truck shouldn't have taken more than thirty or forty minutes to get here, or at least a survey ground drone, something."

Insight told him it had been seventy-four minutes since the train stopped. Accounting for the techs being on lunch break, it meant someone should have shown up. A knot was forming in his gut.

The marshal brought his prisoner out of the car and helped him down. The pasty-faced young man squinted at the sun and grimaced. He appeared to be shaking cramps out of his legs. "Quite the bit of excitement."

The marshal's expression soured. "There's people hurt and one dead. You have five minutes before you go back in the car."

"A luxury. You, Sir Marshal, are a true cavalier among law enforcement agents. But it has gotten stuffy on board without the climate control engaged." The prisoner grinned at Miles and Dawn. Offered his cuffed hands. "Paxton Walker the Fourth. Indisposed, but at your service." When no one shook the hand, he added, "Very wise, very wise. Bad company ruins good character. Let me put your quiverings to rest, my good sir and lady, for this is but a minor matter and my present company the circumstances of ill fortune."

"He's a con artist," the marshal said. "And that's enough exercise. Get back on board."

Before Paxton could approach the ladder, several passengers were climbing down.

A balding man wearing a derby and brown vest accosted Barma. "What's the news, Marshal? It's getting hot in there and it's broiling out here."

"The engineers are working on it."

"And what about our safety?" a woman asked. She had a large toddler in a baby carrier strapped to her front. "Are those bandits truly gone?"

Miles suspected her child old enough to hold down an apprenticeship. Other passengers added their voices to the confrontation. Some took on a shrill tone as Marshal Barma tried to answer. But he kept getting cut off.

"Is someone summoning more marshals? Seraph security?" "If the train resumes operation, who gets to ride in the intact cars?" "Why are the communication networks down?"

"One at a time, please!"

While the marshal might have been imposing one on one, against this kind of crowd, his gravelly voice was fighting an uphill battle and losing. Miles had spent worse times watching a scene go sideways. Dawn appeared content to let the marshal be the front man as she eased away from the center of the crowd.

Miles left them, walking a train car's length away where he took his seat again on the concrete and tried to find a position which would make writing comfortable. But his concentration was shot as he once again considered the blank card. At least he could begin by writing his son's name.

He scratched out the symbols with care.

But he was distracted.

Nothing that was happening on the train was his business. He was supposed to be composing his final message to his son. Owed it to him. The gang of cyborg thieves? A drone bomb? Crowd control and managing a group of panicked travelers? Let the marshal and the train staff handle it.

Work and duty had cost him and his wife Seo Yeun so many days, evenings, and weekends that their son Dillan had drifted. When Seo Yeun was alive, together they couldn't salvage their family. And after her passing, Dillan wouldn't speak to Miles.

"A bit of longhand, I see," Paxton Walker said. He had slipped away from the marshal and sat amiably next to Miles. "A rare art form. Is that Chinese script?"

"It's none of your business."

Hands still cuffed, Paxton waved away the comment. "Of course it isn't. I'm intruding. You'll pardon my manners. Our situation has forced ourselves upon each other. I'm content to sit and enjoy our shade in silence." Two heartbeats later, he continued, "But I am an amateur artist when it comes to matters *langage de fantaisie*. A missive to a lover? A wife, perhaps?"

Miles put the card away, irritated that he couldn't ignore the man, and realizing he was still on edge from the shootout and explosion. The crowd around the marshal had only grown as more passengers from the starboard side of the train had come around to join them.

Dawn and one of the porters walked past. She now held a pair of binoculars and climbed up a train car to scan the horizon in either direction. Her grave expression only grew bleaker.

"And what do you suppose she sees?" Paxton asked. "Or in this case, it's what she doesn't see which should concern us."

Miles couldn't help but answer. "As you might have heard, it's her train, apparently. Once the marshal sends everyone her way, she'll need to have answers."

"I would watch out for that one."

"What do you mean?"

"I mean I saw over several shoulders that she had a picture of you on her device. An admirer, perhaps?"

The knot in his stomach either was growing or it had a friend. "Something like that, I'm sure."

It could mean anything. Perhaps Dawn Moriti was who she claimed to be and kept herself occupied by running security checks on Herron-Cauley trains. Or someone knew where he was and where he was going and put the word out. If so, who else might be waiting for him in Seraph?

The marshal broke free from his inquisitors and made a beeline for Paxton. "Back on board."

Paxton sighed. "And it was turning into such a pleasant afternoon. You don't have to get up for me, Mr. Kim. I know my station. But if you find yourself able to procure some green tea on ice, I can be found at my seat."

Miles wiggled the pen still in his hand. He tucked it next to the card. Then he got up and waited for Dawn to finish her survey of the desert so he could learn how stuck they were.

Chapter Five

"We're going to have to get off the train and head for one of the substations," the chief engineer said.

Judging by the man's set jaw and apologetic eyes, this was the only option on the table, as far as he was concerned. And as the middle of the afternoon had only grown hotter, the thought of walking any distance in the heat was a daunting prospect.

"How far?" Miles asked.

"Closest marker puts us twenty klicks out. They stopped us almost dead center between substations."

Another check in the meticulous planning column on the part of the bandits.

"No point in wasting time," the engineer continued. "I'll send Libby here while we keep working on fixing the train."

One of the two assistant engineers had already donned a hat and began rubbing lotion on her nose and neck. Miles sized up the young woman. Early twenties and about the same age as his son Dillan. He said, "With the bandits out there, going alone sounds like asking for trouble. I'll join her."

"Out of the question," Dawn said. "You're not an employee of the train, but a passenger. I'll ask a couple of the porters to join Libby. If they stick to the shade of the rail line, they'll see any trouble coming."

"Like snipers with burners or flying bombs? She's just a..." He stopped himself. Libby looked old enough to have graduated college or engineering school.

"Herron-Cauley doesn't hire children," Dawn said. "And we have an obligation to keep our guests safe."

Libby spoke up. "I can make the walk. It's not that far. I'll take extra water and be careful."

"Good girl," Dawn said. "With the two porters traveling with you, you'll be safe. We can check the train for any bicycles someone might have stored."

There were no bicycles. More than half the passengers were now languishing outside the train, some taking shelter in the ruins of the shattered luggage car.

A few had set up makeshift shade with propped-up garments. Shimmering heat rose in waves, twisting the ridge like a kaleidoscope. The scene held an unreal quality, as if the train were a crashed ship on an alien world. But this was Earth. Its departed children had returned to it without welcome and were now paying the price.

Miles thought at the last moment he might still join the expedition to the substation. But Dawn remained close by, and he needed to learn if there was something to Paxton Walker's warning. *Watch out for that one.*

If Miles had a price on his head or a warrant for his arrest, he had to know. If Libby and the porters contacted a delayed train company repair crew, they'd return and find some way to bring everyone back to Seraph. And who was waiting for him there? Not much he could do about that for the moment.

He had more immediate concerns. Perhaps it was his nagging paranoia, but he didn't think the danger the waylaid passengers and crew were facing was over. Seeing the three train employees grabbing water bottles and making a last-minute retying of their shoes, he realized he couldn't just stand by and wait.

Miles scanned the track ahead of the train but couldn't make out anything. Besides heatwaves, a dull haze clung to the ground as if particulates from the explosion hadn't quite settled.

The chief engineer and his other assistant went back to work in the locomotive.

Libby and the two porters said their final goodbyes.

"I'm going with you," Miles said.

Dawn heaved a sigh. "I thought we settled this. They'll make the substation by sundown at the latest. I'm sure the company has sent a rescue team our way."

"I'm no rail employee, but as you probably know, I've got over forty years' experience as military police. If you don't trust me to be out there with your people, then you come too."

"It's not a matter of not trusting, it's—hey!"

Miles plodded after Libby and the porters. Stepping out of the shadow of the train felt like strolling from a sauna into an oven. Walking beneath the elevated track provided little shade as the sunlight was hitting at an angle.

Dawn caught up with him. "Do we have to walk so quickly?"

"If you want to make the substation by sunset, yes."

She kept up. He let Libby set the pace, and before long they were all stripping off their coats as the merciless sun beat down on them.

Chapter Six

Something lay in the scrub away from the track. At first it appeared to be a trick of the shadow, dark stones among the brittlebush and cholla, but a quick zoom in confirmed that it was more than that.

A growing dread ran down Miles' spine. "Let's take a break."

Libby appeared to want to continue, but she and the porter waited in the shade of a rail buttress as Dawn followed Miles down the slope of the track.

"What is it?" she asked.

"Trouble."

They had walked perhaps two kilometers. He was feeling it in his hips and found himself hoping for a quick rescue. The train was supposed to be the newest, quickest way to get to Seraph from River City, much faster than the electric rails which ran southward through the farming belt before catching a bus or land freighter for the slower drive west. As Meridian was only just thawing on its attitude towards New Pacific or the neutral free town of Seraph, it had taken some behind-the-scenes wrangling on the parts of business interests to allow for the expansion of the transit system.

The body of a man lay in the prickly bushes. He wore a light blue mechanic's coverall. A hole was burned in the side of his head. Dark patches of sweat marked the dead man's underarms.

Miles stepped through the scrub to get closer. The corners of the man's mouth remained moist. Contrary to common belief, a burner wound could bleed, although this one didn't. Blood had seeped from the man's ears and mouth. Thorns had caught one sleeve and held his hand up in the mock approximation of him trying to ward off a blow which would never fall. The desert would take him and leave his bones there, forever fending off his unseen attacker.

Dawn kept her distance. "What happened?"

"Burner wound. Was he with the rescue party?"

"Looks like one of the rail line workers. Check for ID."

The man had a badge card clipped to his pant pocket. Gordon Lee, Herron-Cauley senior tech. Besides his name, job title, and the company logo, the card held a holographic watermark and an information chip. Miles handed the card to Dawn, who scanned it with her phone.

"Substation twelve," she said. "That's where we're going."

"And he made it this far. It means he was deployed not long after we got stopped." Miles patted down the pockets. No device. "I'm guessing he didn't walk. Think he was alone?"

"It's possible, but not likely. Company wants this train running perfect, so they doubled all the shifts during the shakedown and extended them for six months. Another couple of weeks, he might have been one of two people manning the station, but not now."

Miles backed out of the brush and began to walk a circle around the dry vegetation. "Keep your eyes open for tracks. What kind of vehicle would he have?"

"Electric four-wheel. Track gets twice-a-day inspections, either in person or via drone."

A white coordinate marker stood beyond a rise in the ground. The flat, unpaved road ran parallel to the tracks and ran off in either direction. After a quick check, Miles confirmed there was no one in sight. But no vehicle either.

The loose dust showed tire tracks. While there were marks off the road around lumps of talc and patches of sandstone, it was impossible to decipher what had happened. Miles had a good guess, however. The mechanic had been shot and his vehicle stolen.

Case closed.

But had it been the Metal Heads or the bots? Had Gordon Lee run afoul of the robbers as he drove towards them? Or had he been intercepted by someone who knew he was coming?

"So what do we do about him?" Dawn asked.

Miles caught a tone of condescension, as if after everything they had been through, she was indulging him. He replied, "We continue going. Find a radio somewhere and let Seraph and Devil's Bridge know what's happening."

Libby was calling for them from up by tracks. Waving.

Miles hesitated for a moment before leaving the body. Simple dignity would see the dead man covered and taken out of the weeds. But there was no helping it for the moment. They jogged towards the tracks and climbed up onto the railbed.

"What's wrong?" Dawn asked.

"Gunshots. Did you hear them?"

Miles hadn't, but with the added elevation, Libby no doubt had a better chance at catching any sounds carrying in the hot air. Plus his own ears were still ringing and his cybernetic ear's noise reduction was on overdrive. He canceled the noise reduction and listened.

"Which direction?"

She pointed back the way they came, back towards the train some two kilometers behind them.

"You sure?"

Both Libby and the porter nodded.

"Four shots," Libby confirmed.

One or two blasts of the hand cannon might be a signal from the marshal. But four in rapid succession? They had hours of walking ahead of them to get to the substation, with no way to know if they'd find anyone. And with the discovery of the dead train tech, Miles felt less confident about their current mission.

"We need to know what's going on," he said.

Dawn gave a final look in the direction they had been going. "Lead the way."

The train lay ahead of them like a sleeping serpent reclining on a rock in the hot afternoon daylight. The sun drooped low to the west. Bright orange clouds dotted the sky. Heat radiated from the stones and concrete of the railbed.

Miles had given up trying to run. His calves ached and he felt a stitch in his side. The others had gained a lead on him until Dawn stopped them.

Libby drank from her water before handing the bottle around. Miles was the last to partake. The lukewarm offering could have been bathwater, but at that moment, ambrosia in his parched throat.

Thirst quenched, Miles zoomed in on the front of the train. Nothing moved beyond the veil of heat. Where was everyone?

The ridge to the east appeared clear. So unless the passengers were beneath the train, they had to be on board.

He took another moment to catch his breath so he wouldn't sound winded. "I'll go forward alone."

Dawn cleaned the lens of her binoculars before surveying the train. "You think it's any safer out in the open?"

"No. I just don't like surprises, and we don't know what's waiting for us."

"We'll stay behind you, but no one stays back. We're too exposed. Let's go figure out what happened."

They approached the engine together. The window to the control room was tinted dark and reflected the sky and sunlight. On the ground near the dropped down ladder lay scattered a half-eaten sandwich and a spilled water bottle. Maybe the chief engineer and his people were slobs, but something felt off.

Miles motioned with a finger to his lips. Climbed the ladder. He had to squint to see inside the dark compartment. Before his eyes could adjust, a large shape rushed towards him and struck him in the chest. The marshal, and he had kicked him. The blow sent Miles reeling back, falling from the ladder and landing hard on the ground beneath the train.

The marshal emerged from the hatch and swung down. Miles rolled out of the way to avoid being landed on.

"Where is he?" the marshal barked. He grabbed Miles as he got up, catching him with an unexpected backhand, which shook his head and jaw and almost knocked him back down again.

Miles asked, "Where is who? You mean Paxton? He was with—"

The marshal swung again, wielding his hand cannon like a club. But Miles was ready for him and deflected the blow, slugging the larger man below the ribs with a punch that would have sent a smaller man down.

Recovering quickly, the marshal appeared to be gathering himself for another assault. "Where'd you take him?"

"I have no idea what you're talking about. Take who?"

"Marshal Barma, stop!" Dawn shouted. "What's happened here?"

The large man's eyes darted between her and Miles. He was panting.

Miles had been so focused on defending himself he only just realized the marshal had spattered blood covering his shirt.

"We've been walking or running since we left," Miles said. "We made it a couple of klicks out when we heard the gunshots."

The marshal's voice was a bone-dry rasp. "I told you to stay put so I could keep an eye on you."

"We were heading for the closest waystation. You weren't around to ask permission."

"Miles was with us the whole time," Dawn added. "What happened?"

"They took him...the chief engineer."

Libby and the porter had been watching in silence. But then Libby pushed past them, heading for the ladder.

"Don't go up there," the marshal said, but he didn't move to stop her as she climbed up into the train.

Libby screamed.

Miles bound up after her and almost collided with the young woman. Before them lay the body of the other junior engineer. Blood pooled on the floor and clung to the walls of the compartment in swathes. He appeared to have been torn open.

Miles maneuvered past Libby and went forward but found no one else aboard the engine. He escorted Libby down the ladder and joined Dawn and the waiting marshal. The porter stood back and was chewing his thumbnail.

"Who took him?" Miles asked.

The marshal had a hand on his side where he had been struck. "Someone in a forward car heard a short scream. By the time they got me, it was over."

"I'm sure your con man is dangerous, but maybe you need to focus on what's happening here to the people of the train."

"Don't give me that. I was taking a whizz. And it's a big train. I can't be everywhere."

Dawn cleared her throat. "Gentlemen, the train needs all of us. There's a lot of scared passengers. It's going to be dark soon, and we still need to find a way to let Seraph know our situation."

Libby was wiping her eyes with her sleeve. "Why did they take him?"

"There's too much we don't know," Miles said. "I don't want to wait here until they decide to attack again."

"There's something we agree on," the marshal grumbled. "So head for the waystation again?"

"We'll have to. But I want to look around. They must have left tracks when they took the engineer. And why him and not the assistant?"

"Maybe he fought them and got killed for his efforts."

"You check on that. I'm going to look around."

"Uh-uh," the marshal said. "I'm going where you're going. I don't want you out of my sights."

"Suit yourself," Miles replied. "But unless we're getting everyone out and walking, we'll have to lock these train cars down in the meantime. It's going to be night soon."

Chapter Seven

Trying to figure out what had happened in and around the engine car while the train might have any number of assailants lurking in the surrounding desert was like fighting a fire while a pyromaniac kept throwing gasoline onto the blaze.

For most of Miles' years as a Meridian military police officer, a scene like this would get locked down and a detective would be summoned. There'd be security and a perimeter. Spectators would be kept at a distance. And you would know in your gut that the crime was over and it was time to piece together what had happened.

He'd seen his share of murder sites: low-level crimes which had escalated, robberies where the victim had decided to fight or the criminal had gotten twitchy, and domestic scenes where one or both parties had been angry or high or both.

But this?

Someone or something had climbed aboard, slaughtered one man, and abducted the other. Brazen. Fast, too, judging by the marshal's statement. And the perp, be they man or bot, was still out there and might be close.

The assistant engineer had defensive wounds on his arms and hands. The attacker had used a sharp weapon like a knife. Or, if the assailant was anything like the bots on the ridge which had been shooting at them, simple scythe attachments or perhaps multiple blades, which fit the scene perfectly. The notion chilled him.

This avenue of thought led to the next conclusions. If the bot was automated, it had been programmed to perform this slaughter. If it was a remote drone, someone piloted it here and murdered the assistant engineer before kidnapping the chief. And there was no reason to conclude there had only been one bot.

The marshal stood at the hatch. "Well?"

"You'll need someone with better skill than me to know the particulars, but the attackers were fast, used hand weapons, and weren't concerned about leaving a messy crime scene."

"You're not telling me anything I can't see."

"The answer to what happened isn't here. Let's go outside."

The reddening sun touched the horizon. The air clung to the ground and radiated from the rocks and concrete. A singed chemical smell lingered from the earlier explosion, with no breeze to blow clean air around the train. Added to that was the distinct metallic tinge, which Miles couldn't shake. The blood. A unique odor, and a bad one.

Dawn waited for them at the bottom of the ladder. Her phone was put away. "We can't just wait to be ambushed again. If the substation to the south was attacked, then we should backtrack and go north. Make it to the other station."

"It's not a bad idea. But you won't get everyone to leave. There's the injured, and I'm sure you have some older ones and disabled who can't walk that far."

"But you can. So we go together and take a few people with us. We leave Libby in charge of the porters. They lock down the train, and we make it back by morning with armed guards."

Libby was nowhere in sight. But neither she nor any of the train employees were equipped to deal with whatever had gotten on board the engine car.

"There's a third option," Miles said. "I go after whoever's attacking us."

"It's a big desert out there, and we don't have weapons."

"Then get a group together for the substation run," Miles said. "At the very least I'll be a distraction and will buy you some time."

"I want you with us."

"And I wanted to be in Seraph by this afternoon. You've got more passengers than me to look after. The light's dying. Take care of your end of it, and I'll do what I can here."

She was about to reply but stopped herself. Afraid to show her hand? If she tried to give him orders, it would be obvious, and if she was who she claimed to be, the other passengers needed to be protected, comforted, and told what to do.

The woman in the plaid suit marched their way. She gave them all a look, the creases in her face deepening. Her bow tie hung loose, draped around her unbuttoned high collar, but she still wore her suit jacket. She took a moment to dab her brow. "Have we decided who is in charge of this debacle?"

"We're doing our best to take care of the situation, Mrs. Fish," Dawn said.

"That's not good enough. I understand there's been more violence. We're not safe."

"That's why the porters have instructions to keep everyone on board until we're rescued."

"The porters? They're baggage handlers. I heard the expedition to the sub-station came back without results."

Dawn's tone was that of a professional feather de-ruffler. Hostage negotiators took decades to sound this soothing. "There've been complications. We're about to set out again. We're doing everything in our power to care for your needs. Now if you'll please—"

Mrs. Fish waved her away. "I don't need to hear your platitudes. I need results. When is this next expedition heading out?"

"Within the hour."

"Then I'm coming. Someone needs to take charge of this embarrassing incident."

"It's a twenty-kilometer walk."

"And I do a hundred laps in my pool every day. Daylight's wasting, Ms. Moriti, and the sun is about to set. I'm not spending a night cramped in a train car. Gather your people so we can get underway."

"There's the issue of liability. Setting the dangers of the day aside, the way might prove treacherous."

"I own part of this train line. I'm not going to twist an ankle and sue, if that's your concern."

Dawn's smile was fixed to her face. "Let me go find the junior engineer. She'll lead the team."

Mrs. Fish accompanied her as she walked off.

"I'm guessing the first-class compartments are pretty plush," Miles said.

The marshal grunted affirmatively. "Beds and private water closets."

"We should seal the engine car. I'm going to look around."

Miles slid down the railbed to search the ground for any fresh tracks, be they from tires, horse, or bot. In the shadows, it wasn't possible to tell what was new. But the few traces he saw headed back towards the ridge, where the bandits had come from and where they had fled to.

"Anything on infrared?" the marshal asked.

"I'm not a combat model. I'm heading to that rise over there where the bots had lined up while there's still some light."

The evening held a blue glow as the first stars appeared. Miles regretted not taking some water, but they'd lose the last of the light if he delayed any longer.

Up on the ridge, the disabled bots were gone. The lump in his stomach grew heavier. Each shriveled tree and bush held its own shadow. A hundred mechanical spiders might be out there watching. He zoomed in and scanned every square meter of what he could see, desperate for any sign of more snipers or the machine which had taken the chief engineer.

A lingering puff of dust hung in the air down the opposite side of the ridge from the train. Could be nothing. He pointed. "Any bullets left?"

The marshal had his weapon out again but wouldn't answer.

"Look, I have nothing to do with this. Somebody collected the broken bots, and I think whatever attacked the engine took the engineer this way, possibly in the same direction where the gang fled. But I see something out there, and I don't want you getting nervous."

"Just worry about yourself."

Miles had rarely worked alone. When dealing with genetically enhanced or cybernetically modded soldiers on a bender who needed a time out, you take a partner and backup. Miles hadn't made up his mind on the marshal yet and could only hope he had a steady hand when they found the things which were hunting them.

Chapter Eight

A quad bike lay on its side in a rutted channel where water had once flowed. A stack of solar batteries was strapped to its engine. It had a trailer hitch, but no trailer. The bike's mostly plastic body was a dull green. The cooling fan was still whirring away, and Miles guessed the engine would be warm to the touch.

Neither he nor the marshal spoke. Both surveyed the growing gloom around them.

Miles began a slow walk around the scene. The bike hadn't climbed up the gulley in reverse, so he ascended to the highest point and discovered wheel marks. The bike had been riding along a nearly invisible track which connected to the service road.

A body lay sprawled among the rocks. Miles steeled himself up for the discovery of another rail line employee. It was one of the bandits, the lanky older man who had accompanied the kid.

Touching the man's neck, he confirmed no pulse. Patted him down. The man had his burner in his holster. The marshal shined a flashlight, momentarily blinding Miles, and they saw a burn mark on the man's ear where the laser had struck him. Direct hit from a burner. Miles found little else of interest. A wallet held no picture ID but did have a few data cards. He handed it to the marshal, who pocketed it. Miles took the weapon and checked the charge. Topped off at ten.

Miles spotted something on the opposite side of the track. "Shine your light there."

The flashlight illuminated a small satchel. The burgundy shoulder bag might be large enough for a tablet or a few notebooks but little else. Miles opened it and let the marshal shine his light inside. Credit chips. There were at least fifty in the bag, not all from the same issuer, and each of the thumbnail-sized squares might hold any number of easily transferable credits.

The marshal picked one up and inspected it. "Looks like someone got his cut."

"And got burned for it. But then whoever the shooter was didn't collect."

"What are you thinking?"

Miles scanned the ground for anything else they might have missed. "I'm thinking this wasn't the gang. Revenge, a grudge, a robbery—those things make sense. If he snatched more than his share and took off, gunning him down and leaving the loot doesn't add up. If he got his cut and left, same story."

"People do stupid things when they're scared. One of the gang shot him down and panicked. That's simple."

"But it doesn't answer any of the other questions. If the gang is divvying its share of the take, why was the train attacked a second and third time? There's more going on here."

"You think?" The marshal put the chip back and took the satchel, going through each pocket. "A phone would be nice. There's nothing else out here. We should get back to the train."

A shimmer in the distance. A faint glow, as if something were moving in the moonlight.

"Turn off your lamp," Miles whispered.

The marshal brushed the grip of his hand cannon. Miles made a show of putting the newly acquired burner into his belt. Gestured, as if saying, "See? There. It's put away."

The marshal's light went off.

The crumbling slope led down to the lip of a precipice overlooking a gully. The ground below widened as it led to a pool of blue where the water glistened. A shack or storage shed sat next to a large frame which rested across an exposed shaft leading into the ground. A mining operation. The desert was full of them. It's what occupied many of the first splitters who left Meridian following the initial resettlement on Earth. Most if not all of these didn't want to exchange one abusive government for another in New Pacific. The infectious independence streak sparked a boom during the past decade. It had caught up his son even as Miles fought to grasp the desert's appeal.

Mining was often an excuse for such migrations, and the notion wasn't completely based on the romantic notion of striking it rich.

Before the time when Earth went fallow, some idiot dropped a big rock on the planet. Fragments fell around the area, which would become Seraph. The rock was rich in platinum. And precious metal became the basis for trade when credit chips were hard to come by.

The marshal squinted. "I don't see anyone."

"That doesn't mean there's no one there."

"I'd feel better about this during the day. Just because you don't have night vision doesn't mean they don't. Besides, I don't fancy breaking my neck figuring out how to climb down there in the dark."

Miles didn't argue. As exposed as the train was, at least there they had cover. With a functioning burner, he could keep watch until help arrived.

They began to head up the incline towards the road.

Miles caught a flash of red near where they had found the crashed quad bike. "Look out!"

He grabbed the marshal and together they dove to the ground. A beam flashed, followed by the telltale *snap* of a burner discharge. They crawled towards a stony ditch. Burrs and thorns pricked at Miles' skin and face. Another blast powdered a rock just above him. The ditch gave little cover. He led the way, slithering and scraping through the rocky channel even as more burner fire peppered the ground.

Stopping meant dying. If the sniper, be it a robot or bandit, had company, they could easily be flanked and murdered.

The ditch led to a thicket of tall, prickly thistles. From here, he dared crawl faster. The marshal wheezed as he stayed on Miles' heels. Then they came to a large boulder and a drop-off. They were right above the mining site.

Miles tried to remember how many seconds since the last blast, but his mind was too addled. Unwelcome estimates clogged his vision, along with other distracting data points irrelevant to the situation.

Insight off. The feed vanished. His vision cleared.

The marshal fumbled with his holster.

"Save it," Miles whispered. "We're climbing down."

Not waiting for the marshal, Miles went up and around one side of the boulder, sliding and swinging his legs around and easing himself down. But as his hands gripped the outcroppings of soil, it broke free. Falling. His heel caught hard ground and he tumbled, somersaulting end over end until a final jarring impact stopped his plummet.

He lay on hard ground. His tailbone ached and his elbows and knees radiated pain. The marshal slid down in front of him with unseemly grace, one leg before him like a human toboggan. He was shaky upon rising. Together, they managed to stand and hobble towards the shack and the structure around the vertical shaft.

Once behind cover, Miles fought to catch his breath. Listened. Pulled the bandit's burner from his belt and tried to hear anything beyond this own raspy panting and the wheezing from the marshal. The lawman had his hand cannon out and was scanning the cliff above them.

The gulley was surrounded by the walls of the precipice. A narrow trail led up roughly in the direction of the road. They were trapped. If their attackers kept to high ground, he and the marshal would have no protection.

Head low, Miles checked the shack. Besides a rotted bedroll and some old food containers, it was empty. The faux wood construction material appeared to have been salvaged from a modern building site. He could only wish the shack was made of real wood, as the composite would melt under laser fire.

The pool looked shallow and was nothing more than a glorified puddle which escaped evaporation due to the cover of the ravine walls.

That left the mine as their only option. The frame around the shaft had a chain and pulley which might have connected to a basket somewhere down in the pit. Perhaps large enough for a man, but no doubt used to haul up equipment. A quick check confirmed a set of descending metal rungs which appeared solid.

"Don't even think it," the marshal said. "I'll...I'll distract them, and you do your thing."

"If there's one shooter out there, it might work. We don't know where they're going to pop up. And unlike the train, they're not just trying to distract us."

The marshal nodded as he frantically gazed about at the edges of the cliff. "We should have stayed on the train."

"Yeah." Miles eased himself over to the side of the pit. Tested a rung with his foot. Solid. Same with the next two. He paused. From somewhere above them came scurrying, metal on stone. The soft *ting-ting-ting* could only mean their pursuer wasn't human. But then from the opposite side of the gulley came more of the sounds.

Ting-ting-ting. Ting-ting-ting.

It wasn't a single drone. It had company, and their position was lost.

The marshal wasn't waiting. Perhaps he had heard the bots, too. He began climbing down, his boots threatening to squash Miles' fingers if he didn't descend the rungs faster.

Miles tried to plant each foot firmly to avoid slipping. But then his left boot couldn't find its purchase. No more rungs. The dangling chain hung loosely next to him. No basket, no elevator. He was certain if he gripped the chain, it would pull free and fall on top of them.

The marshal didn't slow his descent. Miles swung down, holding the final rung with his hands, his toes desperate to touch ground.

He felt nothing but air. "Wait—"

The marshal made it to the second to last rung, then slipped, slamming into Miles and sending them plummeting.

Chapter Nine

Hard earth lay far enough beneath them to knock the wind from Miles' lungs and send a jarring shock through his bones. Then the marshal landed on top of him.

Miles shoved, but he was too weak to do more than pat the buttocks and legs sitting on his head. Finally, the marshal rose and switched on his flashlight. Miles coughed and spat, and it took a moment for his arms and legs to obey. The marshal adjusted the flashlight, directing the beam into Miles' eyes before playing it about.

The rough-hewn space had canted walls and a ceiling, which Miles could touch with his palms. Supports made from the composite building material lined the walls and ceiling in a descending slope heading deeper into the earth. A wire shelf rack which might have once held tools stood empty, save for a neatly wound extension cord. The air was dry and cool and held a chalky smell.

"Can you walk?" the marshal asked.

The *ting-ting-ting* echoed from above and was growing louder.

Miles motioned for him to lead the way. With one light, it would be hard enough not to stumble on the clumps of dirt and rocks strewn everywhere. They also needed to see ahead of them to not plummet into a secondary shaft. The place had no doubt been built by a small crew or even a single miner with a team of bots. Miles tried not to think about the quality of the engineering holding the ceiling over their heads. But at least here he'd hear and see the bots coming and might stand a chance at blasting them before he and the marshal got shot down.

The sloping corridor took several hard-angle turns, each corner moving past a darker formation of stone. Behind them, the soft glow at the bottom of the shaft to the surface vanished. Anything outside the flashlight beam disappeared into a soupy blackness.

Something in the dust. Water drops?

"Wait," Miles whispered. Even his soft voice felt too loud. "Shine the light here."

The beam revealed several droplets of opaque moisture in the powdery dust. Not water. Blood. And there around them, across the floor of the mine, were hundreds of tiny pockmarks like inverted boils bearing testament to the passing of scores of spiked metal feet.

The bots which had attacked the train had come this way. Were the droplets the chief engineer's blood?

Behind them echoed the sound of something hard landing on the packed ground. Then came the *ting-ting-ting*.

They hurried forward, making it to a second ladder which dropped a short distance to a level room where three shafts headed off in as many directions. But no cover. Again, it was a poor place for them to set an ambush.

The marshal took a moment to inspect each direction. One shaft had footprints. By unspoken mutual agreement, they chose another shaft. After a half minute of navigating the straight corridor, Miles began to walk backwards and aimed his burner behind them. If a bot appeared, he would only have a fraction of a second to fire. If the machine pursuing them had managed to pick off a bandit driving across open ground, it possessed targeting software or had a competent operator who no doubt had aim assist.

Finally, they came to a corner. Miles took cover and sighted down the barrel. "Kill the light."

The marshal switched off the flashlight and settled behind Miles. The man's heavy breathing came in unsteady gasps. The aroma of sweat and soil filled Miles' nose. Whatever cool air had lingered near the mine entrance was replaced by a stuffy heaviness, like a space suit running out of precious oxygen. The total darkness proved disorienting. The only illumination came from the tiny red LED on the side of the burner. But despite being braced on the corner, Miles began to second-guess his notion of direction. Had he moved the pistol's barrel? If he fired without a visible target, would he strike the ground or ceiling?

While leaving Insight off, he activated his eye's aiming function. If the app had been keeping track, it knew direction and where he had just come from. He aimed towards the base of the ladder. While he had no hard target and the app nagged him to reaffirm the bull's eye before firing, he at least had a sight picture, assuming his app could be trusted.

They waited.

Combat ground drones could be fast. The spiders with legs were especially terrifying, albeit slower than flying drones or anything on wheels. They moved like their namesake, scurrying, with legs ablur as they charged. The Caretakers'

War had seen them in action on both sides, their feared blades and lasers tearing pressure suits, skin, and limbs apart with ease.

So who had a vault of military hardware here in the desert?

All questions for an investigation Miles wished to have no part of. All he wanted was to survive the night.

Ting-ting-ting.

It was coming. They were coming, he corrected himself. As the sound grew louder, the number of metal feet became too many to count. With the flick of a thumb, he switched his gun off and ducked behind the corner.

The marshal clung to his shoulder. "What are you doing?"

"Shh. More than one. Maybe more than two. They'll see the light."

How many seconds or minutes passed? His hands trembled. He didn't remember being afraid of the dark, but this was more than night or the inside of a room after lights out. It felt as if no light had ever reached this depth, even as he dismissed the notion as ridiculous. The rational side of his mind understood someone had dug this mine shaft, had worked it, perhaps even spent part of their lives in this hole, but for the briefest eternity he believed some stygian hell had been breached and overflowed into the cramped space in its awful darkness. With every fiber of his being, he wanted to leave.

Would the bots spot them? Could they detect him and his apps or hear their heartbeats, sensing the electric signals from their central nervous system? Probably nothing so subtle. Their breathing might be picked up by adequately sensitive microphones. Their heat signatures would be supernovae against the cool earthen walls.

Miles kept a finger against the burner's power switch. Recalled his wife's face. Thought of his son and why he was making his trip to Seraph and why he needed to live long enough to make it there.

"I have to sneeze," the marshal whispered.

Please, god, no. Miles mentally did everything to prepare himself for the sound, which would essentially be ringing a bell for the spiders to find them.

The marshal held back, making a soft wet sound which might have been him rubbing his nose against his sleeve.

The metallic footsteps receded. Had the bots chosen a different tunnel, or were they retreating? No way to know for sure, but for the moment they were safe. Heading deeper into the mine meant waiting for the inevitable. And if the marshal's flashlight had a solar or rechargeable battery, it was only a matter of time before it gave out and then they'd be trapped.

Miles touched the marshal's arm. "We're moving. Come on."

Step by step they moved back up the hallway, heading for the room with the ladder. Faint echoes of distant noises could have been the spider bots, or might have been Miles' imagination. They would have to turn the light on. But any sound or signal would bring the spiders back, and he wanted to delay that inevitability for as long as possible.

He tried to guess how far they had gone. Were they halfway up the corridor? With no point of reference, any true estimate was impossible.

From in front of them came the softest hum. A servomotor or several, the tiny actuators which moved the individual components on a robot. Just in front of them somewhere.

Miles tried to stop the marshal, but the man exhaled sharply when they collided.

A tiny red light came to life before them. The faint LED might as well have been a signal beacon. One of the bots had been waiting in ambush, and now it would bring the others their way.

He pulled the marshal down to the ground with him, raising the burner and thumbing it on, targeting just below the light. The spider rose. Its feet tap-danced on stone as it pivoted about. Miles fired. Sent two more shots into the thing. The bot reeled and fell, but it was impossible to see what it was doing as its metal limbs began to crash repeatedly against the walls and floor of the ladder room.

A stray laser burst flashed from the bot and struck the ceiling above them.

Miles fired again twice. His aiming app kept distracting him, demanding more information, as it had no target. Too dark. The slow declining whine from the bot sounded promising. The red light vanished. But if the killer drone was dying, it was taking its sweet time. And it had gone dark while waiting for them once before.

He heard faint metal footsteps. They couldn't wait in the middle of the tunnel any longer.

He helped the marshal back up. "Get your light on."

It took a moment to adjust as the marshal shone the beam around on the ground. It was almost painfully bright, but at the same time it felt reassuring just seeing the white light. The bot was indeed down and not moving, twin blade arms splayed before it.

"You got it," Barma said. "We need to leave."

Miles pointed back down the straight corridor. "This way."

"That's not the way out."

"No, it isn't. But more are coming. Now walk faster."

Keeping the light shielded as best as possible, they hurried around the corner where they had first taken cover. Then they began to run.

Chapter Ten

Another ladder took them even lower. Miles strained his ears. If the bots were staying together in a group, they were either moving slower than before or hadn't figured out which of the two remaining tunnels they had gone down. But he didn't want to wait to see if their luck would hold. They needed a place where they could barricade themselves, or at worst, a better chokepoint.

Five shots left in the burner. It had taken five to knock out the single spider bot. Had this one been armored?

They were walking now, careful as to not trip or touch anything which might make a sound. But the light couldn't be helped.

They paused twice to search piles of old equipment in the hope of finding anything useful. Extra batteries would have been nice, or more lights. Miles stumbled a few times, keeping the marshal and the flashlight beam ahead of him. His feet struck multiple chunks of debris, and he almost twisted an ankle in a crack. Not only was his black suit scuffed and torn, but his polished boots now looked like work footwear in the service of a road crew drudge.

They came to a metal ramp which descended to a wide opening where a wall appeared to have collapsed, revealing a gaping space beyond. The interior framework left off, and the rocky ceiling had no braces. A natural cave of some kind, Miles guessed. The ramp was slick and rusted. Descending unburdened would be tricky enough. Anyone trying to shove a load of ore up the ramp would risk life and limb. They both kept a hand on the wall as they eased their way down to the chamber floor.

Moisture clung to the air. Miles inhaled. The dusty smell choking the mine was barely noticeable here. Was that a breeze? Miles felt it on his nose and paused to affirm he wasn't imagining it.

A single tunnel led into the gray rock at the far end of the cave. A piece of machinery stood on one side of the passage. An old generator. But the marshal wasn't waiting for Miles to inspect it.

He directed the light down the new passageway. "This just keeps going and going."

Miles showed him the burner's battery charge. The marshal set his jaw before leading the way.

Water seeped from the walls and ceiling. Broad patches of red formed along each of the miniscule fissures, and where the water flowed to the ground, a soapy white film formed. Past another smaller chamber, the surfaces appeared unnaturally smoother.

Miles ran a hand along the quartz. "Someone's worked this."

"Lots of mines out here, some really old from before."

How it all hadn't come crashing down over the centuries was beyond Miles' understanding. Little else had survived man's departure. If this was it, the mine stood as a sad, wanting testament to their troubled past. But the generator wasn't that old. And the topside shaft had been built by someone since the return.

"And what brought you to Seraph, marshal?"

"I thought we were supposed to stay quiet." After following the smooth tunnel for several minutes, he said, "Family of greenhouse farmers. Some of the first who saw living outside of Meridian was not only feasible but advantageous."

"You didn't get the green thumb?"

"I can plant and grow as well as anybody. But with advantage and profit comes those who would prey on the desert settlers. Seraph needs law keepers. And what puts your sorry backside on the express train from River City?"

"Just wanted to see the country after my retirement."

The marshal made an expansive gesture to the surrounding mine. "Drink it in. So what happened to that last robot? Your deadeye not working down here?"

"Too dark for a target. And whatever's in the mine after us isn't a dummy drone popping off burner blasts indiscriminately. These might be armored."

"Creepers got what they wanted from the train. Doesn't make sense to be hunting us down."

"Taking care of any witnesses, maybe."

The marshal grunted. "Maybe. Or some old legacy unit who didn't get the notice the fight's over and has it in for returnees."

A deep hum resonated through the air, followed by a metallic shudder and squeal. It sounded large, and the clamor echoed for a moment. The direction of the sound was difficult to tell. But turning back wasn't an option.

The marshal kept the light at their feet, and they stuck to a wall as they descended a slope. Dribbles of water formed a steady trickle which flowed down the center of the floor. More mechanical noises broke the silence ahead of them. Miles stepped into the lead and edged ahead, his burner aimed.

Glowing lights flashed against a wall. Something large began moving. Scraping. The hum grew louder as the machine came to life. It was as large as a transport truck, with articulated limbs.

Why had it started? His proximity or was it being controlled remotely?

Starlike yellow and orange bulbs winked on and began flashing. Hazard lights. This was no combat drone but a digging machine. It adjusted its position, planting feet down on the stone floor. Its limbs moved to a surface of the rock, and a deep-throated buzz began. A cloud of white dust erupted from where the bot touched the mine's wall. It began working the surface with a wide apparatus which appeared to be planing or smoothing the mineral face. The fog bank of rock dust clotted the air.

The earsplitting noise made talking difficult. Miles signaled they continue forward, and they edged past the mining bot. Both kept a wary eye on the machine lest it turn on them, but the bot continued in its task, oblivious to their presence.

"That thing on an automated timer?" Barma asked.

Miles shielded his nose and mouth and kept moving.

They came to a split in the shaft. Miles chose a direction. With the bot behind them, they could manage to hear each other, although once again the darkness reasserted itself.

"Why do you think it didn't attack us?" the marshal asked.

"I'm no bot expert, but maybe it has nothing to do with the spiders. Because if it does, then they know where we are."

"Which means we should have blasted it."

"It wasn't attacking. I'm saving my half-battery for when we need it."

The marshal grumbled something, sounding unconvinced.

The breeze reasserted itself, a welcome gasp of clean air after choking on the dust cloud. A branching corridor led to a large elevator, a heavy-duty lift which might accommodate a large machine like they had seen. Miles made a quick examination. The lift had a control panel which was powered down. He hit one of the buttons. Nothing. There was both a key switch and a card scanner, and they had neither. A search through a set of equipment lockers found nothing.

The marshal left Miles in darkness as he examined the elevator. He rattled the cage a few times before opening a sliding grate. Directed the light upward.

"Safety ladder."

He waited for Miles to go first. Miles put the burner away and climbed. The solid hatchway at the top of the ladder led them to the sealed elevator compartment. Once the marshal arrived with the light, Miles discovered a hinged gate leading out. Before opening it, he put a finger to his lips and then pointed to the flashlight. The marshal turned it off.

The squeak from the gate couldn't be helped as Miles inched it open. The faintest light came down from a graded track leading to the starlit sky. A dull haze hung over the celestial bodies, a legacy from the Caretaker War, a sea of fragments and space trash in low earth orbit which had eliminated every satellite in a volatile chain reaction of collisions and separated Earth's population from Luna and the last of the habitats within the solar system.

They emerged into a broad lot surrounded by rock. More machines stood around them. Weather-beaten and sandblasted, the plastic and steel hunkered among rifts of windswept debris.

The marshal plonked down on a steel tool trunk.

Miles surveyed the path leading out to the desert. "We can't stop here. We're exposed."

"And I'm tired. We need to rest. We need water."

"We need not to get burned down by those things."

Miles had led and been led numerous times and had seen his share of fatigue. It required varying degrees of finesse and tough love. Sometimes a barked order or threat would work, other times consideration and kindness. His last commander had used fear and physical abuse to extract the last gram of effort from his flagging troops. But the most memorable had been a turncoat caretaker who had sided with the returnees.

Carol Flag.

The thick-necked redhead never raised her voice above the soft tone you'd use with someone with which you shared a pillow. She'd be there to grip your hand when you were bleeding or help you up by the elbow when stopping wasn't an option. She once got one old fighter in his company who had finally

crumbled mentally after seeing her squad wiped by a drone strike to keep plug-
ging away. Carol had whispered consoling promises to her for five minutes, all
while under fire.

Miles was no Carol Flag. They couldn't count on the spiders not to come
after them just because they had stepped outside of the mine.

He left the marshal sitting where he was, hoping the third option of moti-
vating an exhausted trooper would pay off. No one wanted to be left behind. It
worked. Like a child whose tantrum had been ignored, the marshal caught up
with Miles, his feet shuffling.

They emerged past a cut in a rock formation where the road led into a
desert illuminated in blue moonlight. Stunted trees and hillocks of raised earth
lined the way ahead. Around them lay a field of shin-high rocks, with plenty of
sticker bushes and leg-busting fissures hiding beneath them. A hundred spiders
might be concealed out there. A quick scan revealed no lights or recognizable
shapes, but in the poor light, Miles didn't trust his eye tech.

The cacophony of noise echoing from the mining machine they had left behind them carried from the ground. Then the sound wound down, fading into
a shrill whine and then silence.

Had something or someone switched it off?

Time to move.

They would follow the road, hoping it would lead to either of the substations or circle back to the tracks. Instead, it led them eastward, leaving the mine
and the hill behind them.

Chapter Eleven

Even Miles was ready to drop to the dirt and rest, but he couldn't shake the feeling that stopping meant dying. Something was out there. His instincts screamed it. Distance from their pursuers was their only chance of making it out of the barren wilds alive.

He focused on the next step and tried not to think about how parched his throat had become. It felt as if he had eaten dust as it lined his mouth. He couldn't spit. Somewhere along the line he had lost his coat. The card to his son was in there. He paused to look behind him but saw only the marshal, who almost bumped into him as he followed along in a stupor.

Have to go back, he wanted to say. But even in his mental fog, he knew the coat and the card were gone. He would write another. He hadn't put any of his thoughts down and realized there might not be anything worth saying.

I'm sorry I screwed up your life. I wish I had been there for you, had loved you more, had known you.

Trite excuses, platitudes, apologies—Dillan would see through them all and laugh in his face. Best to make his appointment, meet with the surgeon, and have a delivery service get Dillan the credit chip. From Dad. Short, simple, and no attempt at extracting any kind of conciliatory expression from a son who hated his father.

Had to survive first. Get the marshal and a train full of people to safety. Figure out why a bunch of robots were lingering to commit murder after a perfectly good robbery which should never have been this successful.

He ignored the part of himself that relished the fact that he was so engrossed in the events of the past few hours that he hadn't once thought of his departed wife Seo Yeun, her eyes, her face, her smell, the way she snored and took forever to brush her teeth and wash up before bed.

This was how he lost himself during his shifts. There was always someone to save, one more detail which needed to be logged and processed to keep a case from unraveling, another lead to follow, someone not his son or wife who required a push in the right direction to escape a bad situation. Yet how many of the ones he had 'saved' would leave the safety and care of a hospital or return to an abusive mate once Miles had gone home? Too many. Meanwhile, his own family disintegrated one shift at a time.

He and the marshal walked side by side. Had the ground begun to slope? The slight grade made walking easier, and the soft dirt gave way to gravel.

Lights glowed ahead of them.

The train, he thought dully. But that was impossible. They were heading the wrong direction.

A row of two-floor structures lay sandwiched between a pair of flat hills. Lights shone from several windows. Miles took a moment to stare at the sight to confirm it was real and wouldn't evaporate in the night air or transform into some new mechanical horror before his eyes.

Was that music?

The clinking of a piano was suddenly unmissable, an off-tune jaunty rag like something out of a serial set in another era.

"Where are we?" Miles asked.

The marshal took a moment to work up the moisture to speak. "There're dozens of small settlements. I don't know this one."

They came to a sign at the side of the road. The lettering appeared excessively neat and patterned, with swoops and calligraphy flourishes.

The Place Where We Sang the Night Hymnal

Painted flowers and vines decorated the corners of the sign. A stack of rocks held the signpost in place. But nothing explained the words. Miles dismissed the riddle of it as unimportant. If someone wanted to designate a spot in the desert as sacred, it was their business.

They needed water and rest. They had murder bots chasing them. And if the hamlet had power, they had a means of communicating and calling for help.

A few vehicles stood parked between the buildings. Some had tarps over them. But otherwise, besides several stacks of storage crates, the settlement had no litter. The windows and structures were intact, and the drab faces of each building were crack-free and shined as if freshly printed with whatever sun-protected laminate went into the material.

Miles stepped heavily onto the wooden walkway leading to a lit storefront from where the music played. Through the window, he saw that the interior of the establishment held three round tables set with cloth and a vase with artfully arranged flowers. A bar stood to one side, and a lean figure played at an upright piano. There were no other patrons.

Miles touched the door. It resisted, then a vacuum seal broke and the door opened with a soft whoosh. The piano player stopped. He rose from his bench and stood taller than most men Miles had ever seen. The man's build reminded Miles of the chief engineer who had gone missing: excessively lean and of slight build. Silver clasps on the man's suspenders held a polish, and a turquoise stone on his string tie sparkled.

He gave Miles and the marshal a toothy smile. "Welcome to The Gypsum. Welcome! Welcome! Take a seat!"

"Water and a phone," Miles rasped.

Behind him, the marshal eased himself into a chair.

The piano player rounded the bar and grabbed a clear bottle, which appeared to hold water. "Of course, of course. I'm Mr. Zoon. This is my place. You boys look like you were out in it."

He poured two stemmed glasses. Miles took the first off the bar and swished his mouth. Tasted more sand than water, but confirmed it wasn't anything alcoholic. When Mr. Zoon turned his back for a moment, Miles spat onto the floor before taking a drink, then another, then finishing the glass and reaching for the bottle. The water felt soapy in his mouth. Too soft and needed minerals, perhaps made from a vapor collector or reverse osmosis. But Miles could be choosy another time.

Zoon had a spring to his step as he brought the other glass to the marshal, carrying it on a tiny pewter serving tray lined with a doily.

"Not many come here, at least not this late. I know the local working camps. Which company you fellows with?"

The marshal chugged his glass down in one go. "Not a company. The Seraph Express."

"The new train? The tracks are on the other side of Confidence Hill. Late night for a survey."

"No survey. Trouble. Train was attacked. You have a device?"

"Of course, of course." Zoon patted himself down before raising a finger as if having remembered something. Back behind the bar, he went through a drawer and produced a phone. He tapped at the screen a few times, swiped, and then his countenance fell.

"Out of power. Not to worry, not to worry." He set the phone down on a charger pad. "Will only take a few minutes." He refilled their water. Glanced at Miles and did a double take, not subtle, before scurrying behind the bar.

"Don't worry, it's not contagious," Miles said.

"Meant no disrespect. Just haven't seen an old face job like yours. Not so uncommon otherwise."

"See many of my kind lately?"

"Lots of different sorts among the miners, and we serve them all."

The marshal perked up. "Serve any here the past day or two? Maybe not miners but others in these parts? Anyone passing through?"

"Like I said, lots of different sorts."

"The place is empty. And I'm talking about the last twenty-four hours."

"Today's been quiet, and this evening's been positively dead. Miners work odd hours, spend days under the ground and then show up and this place gets lively. Hoo-eee, yes she does. It's a regular soiree. You wouldn't guess it tonight, but that dance floor gets lively."

Miles set his glass down. "Besides your device, you have any other access to the data networks?"

"No vid boxes. No fiber optic lines. You want the results of the one-day cricket match in Seraph? If folks want entertainment, they've got to pay. So I play. How about a tune?"

"Later. How's that phone charge?"

Zoon checked the device. "Coming along. But no signal right now. Gets spotty at night. You boys might want to let me check you into one of the apartments. Looks like you could use a showering-off, if you don't mind me saying. And I'm saying it. Not that I mind. Why, if I turned away a pit worker or prospector because of a little dirt, I'd be broken and busted. And you can't sleep on an empty belly. I have a few rehydratables cheap: pepper steak, cordon bleu, macaroni and cheese. Or I can even fix you up an omelet. Powdered eggs, but you know what they say about beggars."

Miles kept his face neutral as Zoon prattled. But they couldn't wait forever while the proprietor stalled them in hopes of selling dinner or a room.

Motion caught his eye. He turned to look out the window, but it was too dark. All he could see was their reflection. Yet something had moved past, he was certain. Not moved...scurried. The *tap-tap-tap* on the front walk was un-mistakably something heavy and metal.

He pulled his burner out and went to the window. "Turn the lights out!"

Stupid. So stupid. If the spider drones had attacked a train, why would they stop at coming after them now that they were inside a saloon?

"What's the matter?" Zoon asked. He was coming around the bar.

"Some drones were trying to kill us. Get these lights out."

"Now hold on. Drones, you say? Nothing like that out here. Not saying what happened to you didn't, but how about we calm ourselves before that laser gun hurts someone?"

A face against the window made Miles jump. It was a girl, young, maybe in her early teens, wearing a plain white frock or night shirt. Her eyes were wide, her mouth leering, and as she blew against the glass, her cheeks swelled, and her mouth made a wet flubbery sound.

"That's just Hill," Zoon said. "Hill, you get on back to your room!"

Miles pushed through the door, his weapon pointing at the darkness beyond the overhang. He grabbed the girl by the arm and brought her inside. "Light out now!"

Zoon muttered as he went to a switch by a swinging door to a side room or kitchen. The bar went dark. Enough illumination came from one of the buildings outside, which cast everyone in murky shadow.

The marshal had taken cover besides the table, his hand cannon held ready. "What did you see?"

"It wasn't clear," Miles said, "but I heard it. It wasn't her."

The girl kept wriggling as Miles tried to bring her behind the bar. She began moaning, a wordless protestation. He let her go and she ran to Zoon.

"It's okay, it's okay," he soothed. "You wait right here, Hill. Papa Zoon is going to make sure everything is safe." He left her by the light switch and headed for the door.

"Stay inside, you fool!" the marshal said.

"Gentlemen, please. I can tell you're out of sorts. There's no one outside. See?"

Miles hurried to catch the man but was too slow.

Zoon pushed the door open and stood in the doorway. He made a show of taking a deep breath, followed by an "Ahhh! Sweet night air. Now if you'll please, my other patrons will think we're closed."

The door shut automatically behind him as Zoon came back inside. Miles hugged the wall and scanned the night beyond the glass door. Had his ears been playing tricks?

As if anticipating a question, Zoon said, "Delivery mech strolled past, no doubt. Some of the miners rent storage and work alone and send their 'dog' home to fetch and deliver and even do a spot of shopping for victuals. Desert's full of 'em. You boys get into something that's giving you the willies? Best take a seat and I'll help even you out. Course, the best option is always sleeping it off. Hill here can turn down a room for you."

He flicked the light switch, and once again the bar felt like it was under a spotlight compared to the night outside. Hill retreated through the swinging door to the back, and Zoon followed her.

Miles hadn't moved. Neither had the marshal.

"He's crazy," the marshal said softly.

"Maybe you have to be, living out here. Doesn't make him right or wrong."

Miles stepped out onto the porch for a better look at the single lane splitting the rows of buildings. No shapes, no delivery drones or dogs, no spiders with laser targeting lights. With his night vision spoiled, there were no stars, either. He strained his ears for a hint of what he had heard earlier. After a minute, he went back inside and headed behind the bar.

Zoon emerged with a platter of foil-wrapped treats. "Some rice cakes with filling ought to tune you boys up. Hey!"

Miles picked up Zoon's device from the charger. Saw it was powered on and connected to a voice call which the screen labeled as *Home*. The phone had been on since Zoon had ostensibly gone to charge it, and someone on the other end of the line was listening.

Hurrying now, Zoon cast the platter onto the bar as he headed for Miles. "Put it down."

"Who's there?"

"It's not your concern."

The voice which spoke through the device was dry and raspy. "Are these our new guests, Mr. Zoon? I am so pleased to have visitors. I hope you're making them feel at home."

Chapter Twelve

Miles examined the phone in his hand. "I thought you said this device wasn't working."

"Put it down!" Zoon cried out. "Put it down!"

The marshal moved to grab Zoon and pressed him against the front of the bar, knocking a stool over with a loud clatter.

The voice on the phone was saying something, but Miles ended the call. Whatever strange game the barkeeper had going on could wait. He examined the phone and saw he had a signal. But when he pressed the screen again for the directory assist so he could reach anyone listed in range, especially the Herron-Cauley substations, the phone lock screen appeared, showing nothing but the time.

Zoon kept struggling against the marshal, but the lawman was big and was using his weight to keep the tall man in place.

Miles approached Zoon. "How do I unlock this?"

"You put that down. Put it down! It's mine."

"And you'll get it back. Hold out your hand."

The marshal had to force Zoon to offer his fingers so Miles could try the thumb on the screen. The device didn't unlock.

"Is it voice command?" Miles asked.

"You hung up on him. You hung up!"

"Yeah. Look, this is an emergency. There's some bad machines out there and a train full of people waiting to be rescued. You get your phone back once I make my call. Deal?"

"'You don't call anyone. I call you.'"

Miles realized by his inflection, Zoon was quoting someone. "What?"

"You don't call anyone, I call you. That's what I was told, and that's what I'm going to do."

"Who calls you? Who was that on the phone?"

Zoon chuckled. His smile became a wince as the marshal twisted his arm.

"Answer the man," the marshal said.

"He's the host. He keeps the town running. Tells me to keep it tidy and make the guests happy. That's what I do. That's what I do."

They got Zoon to a chair and sat him down. The marshal kept a hand clamped on the man's shoulder. Zoon trembled. His eyes glistened with budding tears.

Miles crouched before him. "Mr. Zoon, you have a lovely place. You're a good piano player. I'd like nothing more than to kick back and listen. But not right now. We're dealing with an emergency. People got hurt, some badly. They need help. You can help them by showing me how to make a call on your phone. That would make me a *happy* guest. Isn't that what you want?"

"You can't...you can't..." he stammered. "You can't call anyone unless he wants you to."

"This host doesn't want us to? Why wouldn't he want us to help these people? You want to help us, don't you?"

Zoon looked at Miles and the marshal and appeared ready to jump out of his skin.

"He's out of his mind," the marshal said. "Addict, most likely. Someone's got him running this place and gets him his fix as payment. Check on the girl."

Miles went through the swinging door and found a kitchen. Besides a single pan in a sink, the counters and stove were immaculate. It smelled of bleach. The ventilation hood appeared to either be new or had just seen a deep clean. Even the floor held a shine.

"Hill, are you here? We're going to sit down together outside with Mr. Zoon. Why don't you come out and join us instead of being alone in the kitchen?" He checked the pantry and the refrigerator and found her hiding behind a stack of plastic delivery boxes.

Miles crouched and held out a hand casually. "Did you eat your supper? Mr. Zoon brought out some food bars that look pretty tasty. My boy liked the mac and cheese when he was your age. Come on, let's go have some."

She rose and followed but wouldn't touch his hand. She kept her head drooped as she scurried past the marshal to sit next to Zoon. Miles put the scattered wrapped bars back on the serving tray and brought them over. Hill tore into one and began to eat as if she were starving.

Miles brought the girl a fresh glass of water. "Is Hill your daughter?"

"She's all I got."

"We're not going to hurt either of you."

"He will."

"The marshal? No, he won't. Marshal Barma is a Seraph lawman who helps people like you. Are you talking about the man who gave you this phone? The host?"

When Zoon didn't comment, Miles took a chair. He knew he could appear intimidating. With the marshal holding Zoon in place, Miles' appeal would lose some of its pathos, but the man appeared ready to bolt. For the moment, this was the correct approach.

Miles pushed a water glass towards Zoon. "If you're here under threat, we can protect you. Get you help. Take you someplace where you and Hill are safe. But it starts with you and your device."

Zoon whispered so softly Miles almost missed it. "No signal."

"There has to be a signal. You had the line open."

"Yeah. Yeah. To the host. When he wants to talk. But I don't talk to anyone else."

"How do you order food and other stuff? There are delivery dogs, you said. Food gets brought here. What about everyone else in this town?"

"The host looks after us. He cares for us."

"Someone's footing the bill," the marshal said. "We need to see who else is here."

Zoon's eyes went wide. "No! Stay inside the bar. No guests out after dark."

"What about those vehicles? Who has the keys?"

Miles guessed the answer.

"The host," Zoon said. "If he has a job for me, I get the key."

"You're a prisoner here?" Miles asked. "What happens if you leave?"

"We don't leave. We do our job. And we're cared for. We're cared for."

Hill finished with her food bar and fixed her gaze on another. Miles nudged it in her direction. Her mouth gaped and she grinned, as if having received an unexpected gift. This time she peeled the foil wrapper off as if savoring the moment.

"We have to go out there," the marshal said.

Miles found delight in watching the girl eat. "Yeah. I'll go. Keep an eye on them."

"Should lock 'em both up or cuff 'em."

"Maybe. But for right now they're not the enemy. We need to know what's going on here and who else is out there. Have to assume they're listening and watching. So let's not make any new enemies."

"Besides the ones who are already chasing us."

Miles got up and pocketed Zoon's device. "Yeah. I'll check the houses on this side first and make sure there aren't any keys in the vehicles outside. I don't like that big window. How about we all move a table against the wall where we have a little more privacy?"

Outside, alone. A crisp breeze, surprisingly cold, braced Miles' face. He hadn't spent much time in the desert. River City was hot and humid, and the temperature clung to the night and kept things sticky. But this, he could get used to. The air on his face helped wake him up. They couldn't wait all night inside the bar. Metal Heads, spider drones, and now...

He wasn't sure of what to make of Mr. Zoon, Hill, and this town. Things got strange when people isolated themselves. What bizarre game was this 'host' playing? There were plenty of stories of families or marginal communities, sects, and folks clinging to out-of-the-mainstream ideologies striking out and going north or east or too far south to an infected zone or where things got hot with radiation. Of those who survived and returned, they were usually lacking something which society had and they couldn't replicate. But with them came stories. Petty dictators, abuse, and death. As if humanity hadn't lived through enough.

Miles didn't understand it and understood it less when Dillan had gone off to pursue a career in music. While his son hadn't struck out for the wilds with a group of malcontents, he had ended up in the desert, in Seraph, and to Miles it was tantamount to Dillan turning his back on everything the previous generation had sacrificed for. Fought for. They hadn't carved out a slice of livable land to be divided into River City and New Pacific. And with Seraph, Earth's new colony was splitting into thirds.

The building next to the bar had lights on but was locked. Through a window, Miles made out stacks of identical crates, much like the ones he had seen in the kitchen. There was no sign in the window and no indication this was a private home. The windows and a large sliding side door wouldn't open.

He had been shaking the door when he thought he heard something. The crunch of a footstep? He hurried to the back corner and saw nothing. A rough line of flowering scrub lay two strides away from the rear wall, as if the desert was only waiting for someone not to notice before it claimed the one-road town.

He checked a row of light four-wheel desert runners. The subcompact cars had no keys and needed a card to drive. All he needed was one, and they'd be in business.

The next two buildings down were dark, and none were unlocked. He crossed the street. Someone had set up an outdoor table with chairs, which were leaning forward against it as if to keep windblown debris off them. But a heavy layer of grime clung to everything.

A set of exterior steps ascended to the second floor. On the steps, he found a guitar case. Like the furniture, it appeared to have been left in the elements for weeks or even longer. The vinyl or faux hide cover was tattered along the edges, and mold grew up the neck of the case. The clasps were sandblasted and corroded and beginning to rust.

A guitar was expensive, and much more so out here where anything manufactured had to be carried or shipped. But as Seraph grew into its own, those who settled the desert would become complacent with their abundance. Still, out in this remote depot the guitar bothered him.

If it belonged to Zoon or his daughter, then they weren't well enough to care for themselves.

He went up the stairs and tried the door. It held fast. But a pane of glass was next to the latch. He could break in with little effort. He pulled the burner out and was about to smash the window with the butt of the weapon when the stairs behind him creaked.

He spun. Hill was climbing the steps toward him. She was walking with her hands behind her back and a dull grin on her face.

"What are you doing out here?" he asked.

She kept coming. Was almost at the top.

He backed away but the tiny deck left him nowhere to go.

He didn't want to point his weapon at her, but brought it up. "Stop, Hill. Just stop. Why are you out here alone?"

She paused. Broke eye contact. It was as if she were listening to something or someone. Then she fixed her eyes on his. When her hands moved, Miles felt the old reflexes, with the split-second decision of whether to fire dancing on the edge of a razor.

She held out a key card. Smiled wider.

He took it. Turned it over to inspect it. Too large for a vehicle card but it might belong to one of the doors. "Thank you."

He didn't want to think about what he had almost done. His stomach gurgled and grew sour. With the card, he tapped the locking pad. The lock clicked, and he pushed the door in.

The small apartment had a single bedroom and a main living room, with a pullout sofa and video screen. He turned on a light. There was power. He switched on the screen, but only a No Signal appeared in the center. He turned it off again. A quick inspection found a rucksack of personal effects: undergarments, toiletries, a water purifier, a book in Spanish.

Whoever lived there either had dropped off their belongings and hadn't spent a night on the bed where a set of sheets lay perfectly folded, or was meticulous and Spartan to a degree that would shame a monk.

"Who lives here?" Miles asked Hill.

She lingered in the doorway, her fingers teasing the hem of her dress. But she only hummed to herself, as if Miles hadn't spoken.

The card allowed access to the other apartments in the block of buildings. The downstairs units were single-room studios. One water closet with a puny shower stall served them. These also had personal belongings, but none as neat as the first apartment Miles had entered.

And much like that first unit, personal effects were left behind, but no one was home. In a coat hanging behind a door he discovered a credit wallet with ID. Unless all the chips were blank (he couldn't confirm), the miner or tenant had left behind a few months of living expenses.

So much for this place being a robbery ring. So what was Mr. Zoon's game?

No one had left a device behind. No tools or tents, either. Was it possible they all were at work? If they belonged to a single crew, it made sense. He didn't want to assume anything had happened to them, as he didn't know these people and their habits. They might duck in once a week for a shower and shave and a drink at the bar.

A weird town like this had to exist for a reason, which meant the miners worked someplace close enough to make it worth the host or owners or company dropping this town into the desert instead of having its employees drive to and from a larger community.

Unless this host had reasons to stay further off the grid than Seraph or any other village.

Getting paranoid, Miles, he chided himself, the thought quickly followed by the eternal adage, "You can never be paranoid enough."

But the credit chips remaining in the room showed him that Mr. Zoon might very well be what he was claiming. Odd, but that's what isolation and untreated mental illness might do to a man caring for his daughter while out here away from civilization.

In the first dinky apartment in the next block, he found a journal, pocket-sized and slipped into a first-aid kit in a tote bag. The small handwriting was in Tagalog. Miles squinted and turned on Insight. The translation came word by word, excruciatingly slow. Many of the entries were abbreviations. Each was sequestered by a heavy line and had its own date.

J at bar. 08:19 heads ENE 23k, E1k. Last visual 22:40.

D.R. + D.H. at east hole. Visual 13:02-15:05. Problem with sorter?

V, Y, and Company. 4 guards at capped well. No visual on primaries. Delivery dog sent out 09:52.

Forty more entries followed, with the notes returning time and again to J, to D.R. + D.H., and to V, Y, and Company. There were notations indicating latitude and longitude. Insight popped up a map. What it lacked was a You Are Here. But the first line gave him the clue he needed. All he had to do was backtrack from J's last sighting. With Seraph a known destination and the rail line likewise accounted for by his brain computer, he had a good idea of where he was.

He flipped back and forth through the journal, giving it an admiring look. Whoever its owner, they were either a spy, a claim jumper, part of a gang, or a company looking to do some shady dealings or hostile buyouts.

Not my circus, not my monkeys.

But he pocketed the notebook. There were a few shorthand abbreviations he didn't follow, and inspecting a tactile clue was always superior to looking at a mental slideshow in his Insight module.

"Did you know the person who rented this room?" he asked Hill.

She gave him a look and wrinkled her nose as if the question somehow bothered her.

"Not a nice person, huh? That's okay. Looks like they were up to some fishy business. If they come back here, stay away from them. Is that a deal?"

Something distracted her and she was looking off into the night. Let out a titter. Miles wasn't fast enough to see, but a shape rushed past across the rocks beyond the reach of the light. He hit the light switch and crouched, waiting and watching. A person might sprint that fast, but he felt the constrictor in his midsection tighten.

One of the bots. Delivery dogs didn't skulk in the shadows.

He was about to move when a thundering *boom* erupted from nearby. The marshal's hand cannon. Distant glass shattered. The cannon went off a second time, then a third, then silence.

Miles ran for the street, pausing only for a heartbeat to scan either direction to see if anything was moving before racing towards the front of the bar. It was dark inside. A windowpane was busted in, the shattered pebbles of glass scattered everywhere. Miles took cover between the door and window. Listened. Did a quick peek. His eye processed the image. Nothing was moving inside. But one of the tables had been overturned, and the rear emergency exit stood open.

He vaulted through the window and sheltered behind the bar. The aroma of burned chemicals hung in the air. Cordite. Bullet propellant for those who can't afford a burner. He listened again, straining his ears for metal footsteps, breathing, anything.

Silence.

He hadn't consciously pulled out his weapon, but it was fixed in his hand, barrel forward. He searched the bar and then the kitchen. He resisted the urge to call out for the marshal. And where was Zoon?

The stairs to the upper rooms were outside. If anyone had taken refuge up there, surely he'd hear them. He moved to the emergency exit. Peered out back. A pair of tarped-over vehicles were parked up against the rear wall of the bar. Beyond lay only desert.

A dark object rose behind the second covered car. It was a black bot on legs. A red light blinked to life. A laser target, and it pivoted towards Miles.

He didn't hesitate. Fired. The mechanical eyestalk erupted in sparks, and the machine began to screech and warble as it ducked back down and careened about. To his left, another bot scurried past, too fast to hit, and the sound of its feet tromped up the external stairway. He shifted position. Burner fire could cut through the building material as easy as wax. The machine had spotted him. These weren't the stupid stationary drones which had sniped at the trains. He'd need better cover, and the bar was the only solid piece of furniture unless he wanted to corner himself in the kitchen.

But the marshal was still out there somewhere.

A window upstairs broke. The *tap-tap-tap* of the bot's footsteps stopped directly above him. He aimed, careful not to hold his breath so his hand wouldn't wobble, and waited. A laser sizzled and popped as a hole appeared in the ceiling. A second shot followed instantly, cutting into the floor where Miles had first been crouched.

Miles shot at the hole three times. Something shuffled, then came a heavy thud that shook the ceiling. No more footsteps.

He moved. Head down, he used the vehicles for cover. The first bot he had hit was twitching and skittering in circles in the dust. Confused, blinded, or severed from communication with whomever was controlling it?

Didn't matter. It was still dangerous and might fix on him with something besides a targeting laser. One of its legs appeared mismatched, and many of its parts weren't matte black but a gray finish. It also had exposed wires. He filed the details away. But as he prepared to finish the machine off, Hill came running out from between the buildings.

"No!" she cried as she grabbed the bot in an embrace, shielding it from him with her body.

Chapter Thirteen

"Get down!" Miles shouted. "Get away from it!"

Hill let out a wordless moan, a protest as she caressed the damaged machine which continued to sway back and forth as if drunk. Miles did a quick scan. Nothing else was moving. The bot he had blasted through the ceiling hadn't made any more sounds. He hurried to her and tried to drag her away, but she screamed as if he had hurt her. He instinctively let go, feeling his face burn. Gently he took her hand, all the while trying to see if the bot had a functioning weapon among its six legs and body. With his eye, he targeted the power plant, the tiny walnut-sized nut hiding behind the forward legs.

Hill wasn't letting go.

"Where's your father?" Miles asked her. "We have to find him." He pried at her fingers, getting one hand free. But her other hand clamped onto one of the machine's legs. He couldn't risk tucking his burner away. One other option. Despite the risk of shock or shrapnel, he'd have to shoot the bot. He put the barrel centimeters from the power plant.

Hill seized the weapon before he could fire. "No!"

"This thing hurt my friend. It might have hurt your father. It's going to hurt us."

She was stronger than he had guessed, and he had to actively fight to not lose his burner. The machine quieted. It remained standing tall with its targeting appendage tucked in its center. Then it sank down on its haunches.

"Sleeping," Hill said.

"Yeah. It's sleeping. We're going to let it sleep. Let's go inside. We'll get you safe, get something to eat or drink."

When she released the burner, he stumbled back. She began touching the bot, petting it while cooing. One shot, and it would be done. Yet something about the spider's ad hoc construction troubled him. He had seen combat bots explode before, either by damage from weapons fire or design upon malfunction. Kamikaze drones were a simple thing, a mine strapped to a chassis. They needed to get away from it.

Another scan of his surroundings picked up nothing, but that might change in an instant.

"Help me find your father," he told her.

Hill was whispering softly to the disabled drone and ignored him. If Hill had a strange attraction to this bot, it was because she was familiar with it. Which meant Zoon knew the robots too.

He checked the alley next to the bar before heading upstairs. Switched on a light. The bot he had burned lay in a heap of metal. Besides not having a targeting laser, it was identical to the one out back and a quick inspection found nothing explosive. It too had mismatched parts.

The apartment had two bedrooms, one spare and the other cluttered with collected rocks and dried flowers mounted on scraps of wood. He found a flashlight. Back downstairs, Hill remained at the stricken bot's side as Miles went inside through the emergency exit and turned on the bar's lights.

Time to piece together what had happened.

From the knocked-over furniture, something had come through the window and tussled with the marshal. Or maybe also Mr. Zoon. Three shots fired, not four. Had the marshal run out of bullets, or had he been knocked out? No blood. And then someone had exited out the back.

If the marshal had escaped, he hadn't called out or tried to make contact. But with the bot waiting for Miles, it felt unlikely the marshal had won the fight. If the bots hadn't changed their behavior since shooting down the metal head on the quad bike, they didn't bother cleaning their messes. And if the marshal had used his hand cannon before becoming disabled or incapacitated, he didn't stick it back in a holster.

Miles double-checked and confirmed the marshal's weapon wasn't on the floor.

The spiders weren't neat and tidy, but Mr. Zoon was. And someone knew how to fix the machines. Hill's attachment to the injured spider bot only confirmed his suspicions.

This town was a trap, and they had walked into it. Zoon might have been a prisoner, but that didn't mean he wouldn't kill for his master to avoid whatever punishment the host meted out.

No drag marks just outside the door. The marshal was a big guy. Two spiders to carry him. Or maybe three—it was too vague of a math problem. How many killer drones does it take to carry a 100-kilo man? Insight wasn't helping. The more nagging question was: why take the marshal?

They had killed the Metal Head and the assistant train operator, yet had taken the chief engineer. So why the marshal?

Miles started when the device in his pocket chimed. He had forgotten about it, and now someone was calling. Not someone. The host. According to Zoon, the one person in the area who had a data signal.

He hit the button to answer. The line connected.

The raspy voice spoke, now with a purr. "Miles Kim. Lawman, Meridian service. Attained rank of First Sergeant. Decorated. Husband to wife, Seo Yeun, deceased, and son, Dillan."

"Who is this?"

"I didn't know you before; I know you now. I see you."

Miles scanned the night and resisted the urge to retire to the shelter of the bar. "I don't see you. You have the marshal, don't you? Is he hurt?"

"The marshal will be with me soon. You have purpose to me. I have decided to spare your life. I have an exchange which will benefit you."

"This is no way to start a relationship. Let's meet."

"Our communication now is sufficient. You will either answer yes or no. Yes will mean we can pursue a mutual goal together. No, and our exchange will conclude."

Miles looked at the device with renewed suspicion as if it might blow up if he answered the question wrong. "What's the exchange?"

"You had an appointment with Doctor Fanti Hill. A pseudonym, real name unknown. He or she was going to extract your implants, the implants you freed from their digital management held by Meridian. This would allow these units to be sold. Because of the nature of your old Insight module, this procedure would also result in your death."

"How is this any of your business?"

"Because you are beautiful as you are," the host said unironically.

"Usually people ask if there was a tip involved in my last haircut."

"I sense levity. I am serious. You are beautiful, Miles Kim, and I would give you and everyone like you a purpose."

Miles rested a hand on the grip of the burner in his belt. "I have a purpose."

"You have intention. This would be cut short if you had continued on your journey today."

"Is that why you stopped the train and killed all those people?"

"The gang which robbed the train was not under my direction. But I know them and have observed them and once I understood their plan, I implemented my own."

"Which was what, exactly?"

"I too required something from the Seraph Express."

The host didn't elaborate further.

Miles fought to keep his voice calm. This host had hostages and talking to him was like talking to a drunk or someone experiencing a mental health crisis. Miles had to remember his training. No combative words. Don't contradict. Don't threaten to burn their brain with a laser once they poke their head out from whatever hole they were hiding in.

"What you wanted from the train—you're talking about me," Miles said.

"No. I learned who you were once you came after my drones. I want you to help me make a sanctuary for others like us. You have no close connections. I seek like-minded souls who will build with me."

"This is a hell of a job interview. You try to kill me and then offer a place in your desert kingdom for unrecyclable cyborgs? Maybe lead with the soft sell. Let me see the marshal. Then I'll consider your offer."

A long pause followed.

"You still there?" Miles asked.

"Yes. I sense your tone and understand mere words won't sway you. I'll have to show you instead."

Another bot rose from the desert floor, dirt and rocks falling away from its body. Even as Miles dropped the phone and pulled his burner, a red light on the bot twinkled, shifted to brilliant blue, and fired.

Chapter Fourteen

Miles woke with a splitting headache. He lay on his back on a blanket spread on the ground. He had a hard time seeing. It took a moment to realize his artificial eye had gone dark. A crust of soil coated his face, and a soreness radiated through his limbs and up his back.

What had happened?

It felt as if he had been dragged across the ground for a few kilometers and down a flight of stairs for good measure.

A fire burned nearby. Someone had set up a small stove which burned a blue and orange flame. An iron teapot percolated away, with liquid sizzling as it frothed from the clinking lid.

Insight, how long was I out?

His module wasn't responding. He groaned as he sat up, feeling nauseous. Whatever blue light had struck him left an image on his real left eye, a ghost which floated center vision as if he had been welding without a helmet for protection. It felt like sand when he blinked.

He was underground. A low cinnamon-colored ceiling sloped up into the shadows beyond the fire. He tried to get up. Too fast. A wave of dizziness took him down, but he didn't wait to try again. He got himself propped up on his elbows long enough to confirm he had been disarmed. Zoon's phone was gone too.

A figure appeared. The kid. The boy robber with the oversized artificial hand. The kid's burner dangled from a shoulder holster. He had a plastic cup and filled it from the teapot, holding the handle with a rag. The fragrance of rosemary and mint caught Miles' nose and other herbs he didn't recognize.

The kid set the cup before him. "Here, drink this."

He poured a second cup and found a place on the opposite side of the stove next to a pack. From a pouch, he produced two bundles. He tossed one over and unwrapped the second one and started to eat what looked like an empanada.

Miles ignored the offerings. A casual check for anything which might serve as a weapon came up short, except for the teapot. The miner's notebook lay near him, tossed aside as if the kid or whoever had searched him had deemed it unimportant.

"Where am I?"

The kid took his time answering as he chewed and swallowed. "Near the Place Where We Sang the Night Hymnal."

"The words on the sign are the town's name? What do they call it on the map?"

"Don't have a map. What else you going to call it?"

Something shorter. But Miles didn't want to waste time arguing. "Who else is here?"

"Drink your tea."

"You know the man on the phone who gives Mr. Zoon his orders? This host?"

The kid broke a piece of empanada off and inspected it before popping it into his mouth. "I remember you from the train. You followed us."

"Your boss killed some people and left a lot of others stuck in the middle of the desert."

"Not my boss."

"Does that mean you're in charge? That skinny fellow you were robbing our train car with was calling the shots, but he's not around anymore."

The kid stopped eating. "What do you know about Bryce?"

"Was that his name? Did Bryce take his cut and leave your hideout without permission?"

"He stole half the take and didn't want to wait for payout. Some of the boys went looking for him but couldn't find him."

"Someone else found him. Shot him down."

"Then he deserved it for cutting out after ripping us off."

"That's a lot of hardware you've got roaming the desert. Some military-grade stuff. Seraph has a market for mothballed tech from the war?"

The kid ate another morsel and sipped his tea.

Miles continued. "You got away with your loot. So why the drone strike? And why attack again and kidnap the engineer?"

"That's not us. That's the desert ghost. He does what he wants and we stay out of his way."

"So this ghost runs The Place Where We Sang the Night Hymnal?"

"The old coot at the watering hole does. But the ghost probably tells him what to do and I'm sure he listens. If you're not going to eat yours..."

The kid was eyeing the second empanada.

"Be my guest," Miles said.

Without hesitating, the kid took it and wolfed it down. Miles sniffed his own cup of herbal tea. Realized he was thirsty, but set it aside. As the kid wasn't watching closely, he took the notebook and slid it into a pants pocket.

"So you don't work for this host...or desert ghost. But you're helping him keep me prisoner."

The kid shook his head and spoke with a full mouth. "There's the exit." As Miles crawled towards the opening in the wall of the cave, the kid added, "Just watch out for the dogs."

The eroded cavern beyond the small chamber looked like a half-covered garage, which doubled as a makeshift camp and a garbage dump. Bedrolls and knickknacks occupied one side of the space, alongside a few chemical toilets. Heaps of refuse appeared sorted by scrapped chunks of metal, composite material, and machine parts which were further subdivided into tinier piles. Several vehicles stood parked at the periphery, and beyond them waited a pair of horses.

A group of the bandits near the beasts appeared to be holding a discussion. One spotted Miles but no one did anything as he picked his way through the maze of clutter.

Were they going to let him leave?

He spotted his hat lying in the dust near a rubbish heap. He picked it up and after an inspection, put it on. Still no reaction from the gang.

One of the Metal Heads worked near the closest vehicle, an electric lantern burning. A large tool chest stood open next to a dirt bike lying on its side. As he got closer, he recognized Hill. Her face and arms were dirtier than before. Then the bike moved. It reared up on six legs, the drone's damaged eye stalk extended but quivering. The machine appeared to be having trouble and half its legs collapsed, sending it crashing to the ground.

Hill made a troubled sound as she straddled the drone and detached a servo, making the eye stalk sag. Two more spider drones stood idly by, their red eyes half open and watching.

"Are you okay, Hill?"

Her jaw was clenched and she didn't make eye contact as she stepped to a small pile of electrical parts. After a moment of sorting, she found what she was looking for and returned to the damaged drone. Another rubbish heap stood beyond the bike, composed of the ruined remains of the spiders he had shot down. Nothing was being wasted here.

At least the girl appeared unhurt. She knew where to find the parts and tools she needed, and she doted on the crippled machine as if it were a finch with a broken wing. If she left the cave, would the functioning sentry bots stop her, or could she come and go as she pleased? And what about the Metal Heads?

One of the drones perked up as Miles moved past. With a whirr and a series of snaps and clicks, it fell in behind him as he approached the gang members. They all turned to face him. Hard looks, one and all, and each packed a pistol or burner. One of them had an exposed robotic arm, and each appeared to have portions of grafted metal on their ears, neck, or face. A woman at the rear of the group stood on two artificial legs with reversed knees. Miles didn't need his Insight module to recognize a sprinter configuration.

"Which one of you is in charge?"

"None of them, as of the past hour," the host said from behind him. His hoarse voice held a canned electrical buzz.

The spider shadowing him strode past, its unwavering red eye fully open and staring, pivoting on its stalk.

"What happened, besides you bringing me to your hideout?"

"A change in oversight. My friends here have aligned themselves with my view of how things could go for us all."

"If they're with you, did you tell them they're accessories to murder?" Miles asked.

"They understand what commitment means."

Miles kicked a container full of chips and small cables. "This is what you wanted to show me?"

"Part of it, yes. How many of us survive by picking through the refuse of a world which has forgotten them? How many more are afraid to leave service in Meridian because they are unable to free themselves from the software which commands their limbs and organs, leaving them enthralled in service to a master they never chose?"

"You're talking about trading one master for another."

"I wish to be master to none. No one here is beholden to me."

"What about the Metal Head who you shot down?"

"Tolerating treachery is a different matter."

"And the train personnel? The assistant engineer? The rail employee we found dead south of the train?"

"Unfortunate casualties. With the new rail line active after so many delays, I took the opportunity to take something which will guarantee my future, but realized how much more could be accomplished with the assets which presented itself."

"This have something to do with the people you kidnapped?" Miles asked.

"Bloodguilt, which I place at the feet of those tyrants who would exploit those of us who gave our all in service."

"Plenty of people hate Meridian. I'm not a fan. But the rail line is owned by Herron-Cauley. And the marshal works for Seraph. About as far away from Meridian as you can get."

"The rail company is another face of the same creature. And Seraph is no haven. Its agents are nothing but mercenaries who would turn you over to Meridian if the credits are enough."

"And credits aren't what you need, judging by the fact you left a sack of them sitting in the desert."

The host gave an exasperated sigh. "Automation still has its limits. To the matter at hand. There is good you can do. I offer your life meaning. I have access to tools, expertise, and upgrades which you could only dream of as a grunt in Meridian service."

"I was a military cop."

"Yes, I know. Keeping the rank and file in line after decades of duty until you yourself decided to throw off your shackles."

"My jailbreak took ten minutes with a subroutine saved on a flash drive."

"Minimize your efforts, if you will. You were a slave before your liberation. With me, you can help so many more."

And what did the host consider Hill or Mr. Zoon? Were they slaves? But arguing with the madman wasn't going to help Miles, the marshal, the chief engineer, or anyone else waiting on the Seraph Express.

"All right," Miles said. "Let's say I'm in. What do you want me to do?"

"Learn to trust me. I will care for you. Your work will take you to Seraph. From there I will give you instructions. I have assets I can share. You will be my agent in the city and represent my interests."

"Interesting. How about a gesture of good faith? Let me see the marshal."

"No. I have a different use for him. Forget him, and forget those who would stand against us. You, Miles Kim, will be the sole survivor who tells the tale of the Seraph Express disaster."

Chapter Fifteen

The Metal Heads standing around him didn't appear fazed by the implications that the host was going to murder everyone at the train. Was he the only one hearing what this maniac was suggesting?

"Rest until dawn," the host said. "Then I will have one of them transport you to Seraph."

Miles felt hot. He loosened his collar. "I'll need my burner. And my eye isn't working."

"The damage to your eye is temporary and can be reversed. You won't need a weapon here. I mentioned trust. I will have to learn to trust you as well. Keeping you unarmed will prevent any indiscretions."

He couldn't wait any longer. The host was setting his plans into motion and wouldn't wait for Miles to catch a few hours of sleep.

"If my work is in Seraph, then why wait?" Miles asked.

"To prevent you from trying to warn anyone who might come and rescue the poor souls trapped in the desert."

"I don't care about them. You see my face. I've been putting up with looks of shock and pity for decades. Meridian's good citizens have always wished for horrors like me to show them common courtesy and stay out of sight. To hell with them."

"And what if one of the stranded passengers was your son?"

The question gave Miles pause. The host already revealed he knew about Dillan and several other easy-to-uncover facts about Miles. But the implied leverage in the question was impossible to miss. The one person Miles had left in the world was vulnerable. Anyone who could pull off a daylight strike on a train full of Meridian and Seraph citizens could reach beyond their hole in the desert and hurt whoever they wanted to.

"You want to waste my time with hypotheticals? I'd go and save him. But my son's not here."

"He isn't, is he?" the host purred. "To your rest, Miles Kim."

One of the Metal Heads with a lantern led him back to the cave. The soft glow shed enough light to make his way back to the blanket. The kid bandit was already down and sleeping on one of the bed rolls, the stove out.

Miles took the lantern. The Metal Head didn't want to let it go until Miles peeled the man's fingers off the handle.

"I'm afraid of the dark. Your boss wants me to rest? I keep this."

The bandit rolled his eyes, then exited the cave. From the sound of his footsteps, he wasn't sticking around outside, a small relief if Miles was going to escape. No weapon, half blind, with at least three bots and six-plus bandits outside. Plus the kid.

The kid raised his head from his blanket. "Afraid of the dark. That's rich."

"Where do you come from, kid?"

"Told you not to call me that."

"No? And why not? You should be home in bed because there's school tomorrow, not here, not in a dirty bunker with a bunch of criminals."

"Put that lantern out. I'm trying to sleep."

"Are you part of what they're doing? I get making a score. It's got to be tough scratching out a living. But the host is now in charge, and your clan is going to kill all those people by that train. All those folks want to do is make it to Seraph and get back to their families."

"Well, they shouldn't have come through this stretch of desert."

"They didn't know it belongs to you or the host. Should that mistake cost them their lives?"

The kid scoffed. "I don't care about that."

"Then what do you care about? Will you be the one who burns them down?"

"No one's going to burn them down."

"The host told me otherwise," Miles said. "Maybe you don't have to be the one pulling the trigger, but you're part of it. I've seen what happens to people who go down this road. It eats them up, especially the ones who think they're tough. It will stick to you. Sear your insides. Every day, every night."

"You're talking about my conscience. I don't believe in that, either. You're starting to sound like my nana."

"So you do have people. Your nana out there in the desert?"

The kid rubbed his eyes and glared irritably. "Works one of the mining camps. Copper and moly."

"She works the pits?"

"Nah. Hospitality."

"She know where you are?"

"It doesn't matter. Why you asking? It's none of your business."

Miles raised a hand as if to soothe the kid. "Course it's not my business. But if your nana was out there, you wouldn't want to see her get killed just to cover over a robbery."

"My nana would be smart enough not to get stuck like that. And if she did, then too bad for her. Enough sharing time. Turn off that lamp."

Miles dimmed the lantern. "Sure, kid. We sleep while the grownups do the real work."

"What do you mean?"

"Deal with the train. Handle the prisoners. Get me to Seraph. Those are the jobs. So what's yours? Watch the garbage pile to make sure none of it runs off? Maybe you won't have to do any of the bad things since it looks like they're happy leaving you behind to get your sleep. Sounds like they don't trust you since your buddy Bryce stole that bag of credits."

"They trust me just fine," the kid said. "You're trying to get my skin."

"It's *under* your skin. And maybe I am. But I just talked to your boss, and he's already got a job for me. Looks like you'll be the bottom dog of this posse for a while longer."

"What's the job?"

Miles made a show of getting comfortable. Dialed the lantern down to the brightness of a match's flame. "Wouldn't want to take my word for it. Go ask your crew. But the host wants me to go to Seraph, and he wants one of you to drive me. Not sure I trust any of those boys out there behind the wheel. But maybe you and that fancy hand of yours might handle a desert runner. Just a thought. But I doubt they'd give a kid a job like that."

He closed his eyes. Listened as the kid scuffed his way out of the cave. He returned several minutes later.

"What's the word, kid?"

The kid flopped heavily on his blanket and slapped his roll a few times before plopping his head down. Miles knew the early stages of a tantrum.

"You get the job?" Miles pressed.

"Don't want to talk about it."

"They're having someone else drive me, aren't they?"

The kid got loud. "Said I don't want to talk about it!"

"It's going to be all right. Every recruit gets punched down a few times. Tough to be on the bottom rung. Course, they let me climb right past."

"You keep talking, I'm going to burn you."

"You could," Miles said reasonably. "But then they'll do to you what they did to Bryce. That's how the host runs things. Not sure who was in charge before, but now this appears to be a results-based outfit. You want to make points, you got to be the one who gets things done. Hike a thumb back over your shoulder and say, 'Hey, that was me!' I can help you with that, then we can both get ahead."

"You're trying to trick me," the kid said.

"Out of tricks. You heard what the job is. The host wants me to go to Seraph. I need a driver. I'm unarmed, half blind, and I don't want to waste the night lying on my back. My bones are too old for sleeping on rock. So what do you say we take a drive, and you do your nana proud by showing her and your boss you know how to get things done?"

Chapter Sixteen

The cavern beyond had grown quiet. No more voices, no machines moving about, and whatever repairs Hill had been performing had quit for the night.

For someone so young, the kid didn't know how to sneak. While he kept his head comically ducked, his boots squeaked with every step and his breathing was too loud.

Nerves, Miles. Calm down. After a lifetime of facing danger, Miles wished he could keep calm. But his heart hammered, and perspiration dampened his brow. Like a rookie on his first encounter with a perp who wasn't coming quietly. Adrenaline had never been Miles' friend. He had known a few good troopers who could stare down enemy fire with a steady hand. Miles couldn't remember the last time he had faced true danger without his augmentations tweaking his brain, dialing panic to cool-headedness, controlling fear, and pumping ice into his veins.

But not now.

The fact that the kid had listened surprised him. He didn't want to hurt the boy, but he was going to if the kid hadn't agreed to go steal a desert runner so he could take Miles to Seraph. But knocking the kid over the head and making it out were long odds. At least the kid might get them past the bots and the other gang members.

They made their way through the scrap piles, which were the grist of a new drone army the host was building. Could Hill possibly be the only person working on the project? There was too much Miles didn't know. Add it to the list. And the thought of the girl naively slaving for the host in service of his evil designs set his teeth on edge.

A few of the Metal Heads had bedded down around the rocks near the cavern exit. It was only a fraction of the gang. Either they had another hideout, or they were out working.

The closest horse chuffed as Miles and the kid approached. One of the sleeping figures rolled onto their back and adjusted a lumpy foam pad which served as their pillow, only to settle in again.

A machine on the opposite side of the chamber began to hum and whirr, a compressor perhaps, but it shut off just as quickly with a soft sigh. Miles hoped the sleeping men were used to noises.

The kid opened the door to one of the desert runners. The four seats were cramped and could be folded down flat. He hit a switch on the back, which powered the vehicle up.

Miles' attention was divided between him and the slumbering bandits. None of them stirred as the young outlaw got behind the wheel and started the engine. It purred. The kid made an impatient gesture as Miles hesitated. If his assist with the escape was a ruse meant to test Miles' loyalty, he was about to find out. He climbed into the passenger seat.

The kid didn't wait for seatbelts. After putting the car into drive, he rested his right hand on the gear shift, an easy reach to the burner in his shoulder holster.

The crunch of tires was much louder than the electric engine as the desert runner crawled forward and up the curved driveway. Shadows of the surrounding rock formations stood around them, and with the lights out, the bumpy road was almost invisible. The kid was managing as they passed across rolling ground while staying on the track.

"We make it to the service road, then you'll see how good I can drive," the kid said.

A light flashed in their faces. A sentry, maybe more than one, impossible to tell. Miles squinted as the kid hit the brakes. A figure walked towards them as a companion kept the light and perhaps a weapon trained on them.

"Kid, what are you doing?" the sentry asked.

"Taking him to Seraph as ordered."

"What orders? He's leaving in the morning."

"Well, there's new orders. You're not on the same ladder rung as me anymore, Chang."

"We didn't hear anything about that." Chang stooped to get a better look at Miles. Miles smiled at him. Confirmed Chang carried a weapon. "Stay put. I'm going to check with Trevor."

"He'll tell you the same thing. We're going to be late."

"That's not my problem. In fact, turn this thing around and go back inside, and we'll clear this up together. Because I don't like it."

"Hey, Chang," Miles called. "We haven't met yet. The host told me about you. Said I could learn a lot from you and the others. Will I be working with you when I set up shop in Seraph? Because he said you were an expert."

"Did he?"

"Yes. In fact, we'll have to talk soon. But for right now, we're heading out early like the kid says."

Chang moved a split second before Miles did, but Miles' hand was faster. He pulled the burner from the kid's holster and snapped off two shots. Chang howled and fell and didn't get up.

The kid screamed and grabbed for the weapon, but Miles used it to pop him in the nose while pressing the kid's leg down onto the accelerator. The second bandit holding the light jumped aside as they sped past.

They hit a hard bump, sending both Miles and the kid slamming into the runner's ceiling before plonking back into their seats. The kid's face was bleeding.

A pop exploded behind Miles' head as a burner hole appeared in the plexiglass in the rear of the cab. Miles took the wheel and yanked it in time to avoid a rock. The kid twisted his foot off the pedal as he tried to wrangle the burner out of Miles' hands, but Miles was stronger. He got the barrel pointed into the kid's face. Instead of shooting, he reached over and opened the door and shoved. The kid went tumbling as Miles climbed over the shifter and into the driver's seat. Gunned it.

As the desert runner barreled forward, Miles fumbled for the headlights and steered wildly as he was heading straight for an embankment. He bounced over a rut and onto a road, full speed into the night.

Chapter Seventeen

They were coming. Had to be.

Miles didn't see any light behind him, but knew it would only take minutes for the gang to start their pursuit. He kept his one eye glued to the road, scanning for any turns or obstacles and searching for any sign which would indicate what direction he was heading.

The bandits would chase him using the other desert runners, and might also call ahead to any others who might be able to head him off. Of greater worry were the spider bots. How fast could an unburdened spider scamper across the desert? Insight surely knew, but Insight remained offline.

The glow of the Place Where We Sang the Night Hymnal lay dead ahead. Someone had the lights back on.

So the Metal Head hideout was close, a short walk away. With the dark shape of Confidence Hill in the distance, Miles was able to orient himself. The train tracks lay beyond. Not far if he could avoid bottoming out the desert runner and stranding himself.

He cut across a stretch of hardpan, hitting a few treacherous bumps and rocks which jarred the vehicle. He kept his jaw tight to avoid biting his tongue. But as he turned onto the trail which he and the marshal had followed, he knew he would make it back to the train.

Someone in the road.

He swerved hard, almost clipping them, before hitting the brakes and pulling the runner into a sharp skid. A cloud of dust rose around him as he stepped out of the vehicle.

"Dawn? What are you doing out here?"

The train attorney held her arm across her nose and mouth. "Looking for you and the marshal." She held up his black jacket. "I was worried."

"There's no time to explain. Get in."

She climbed into the passenger seat. Miles was about to put it in gear when she put a hand on his.

"Wait," she said. "Where's the marshal?"

"Taken by the bots. There's a bunch on my trail right now along with the Metal Heads."

He started driving. He kept scanning the road carefully.

"Then where are you going?" she asked.

"Back to the train. Get you someplace safe, check on the passengers."

"If they're chasing you, you're going to lead them back there."

He kept his foot down, going as fast as he dared. "Don't you think I know that? I don't have a better plan. Those things are going to kill everyone. We need to be ready."

"How do you know?"

"Because I talked to their boss. He's crazy. He thinks this stretch of desert is his, and he's trying to make a cyborg utopia. Why aren't you with the passengers? I thought you might be with the party heading north to check on the other waystation."

"That was a fiasco. We made it to a junction house two kilometers away, then Mrs. Fish's resolve broke when we found the fiber optic lines were cut. So we headed back. I got a whiff of a signal a few times but it faded before we could call for help. And then you and Marshal Barma didn't return, so I went out to find you."

Miles kept his attention on the road. "We were attacked and escaped through a mine."

"You should have stayed put. Slow down; you're going to take us into a ravine. Now who's after us?"

"Calls himself the host. He's got a miner settlement under his control and the Metal Heads running it. They've got more spider drones, and tough ones. But like the chief engineer, the marshal wasn't killed. He was kidnapped."

Dawn kept glancing at the desert runner's instrument panel. "That doesn't make much sense. But we've got a vehicle and a full charge. We could make any of the substations or even Seraph. There's no point in us going back to the train if we're just hoping for rescue before the gang swoops down on us again."

"And what about the marshal and everyone else?"

"We'll help them by calling for reinforcements. What's wrong with your eye?"

"It got zapped."

"Then let me drive," Dawn said.

They'd go faster if she did. But swapping drivers meant stopping. And why was Dawn so fixated on him? Something about her wandering the night in search of them—him, he was certain—was like having something stuck between his teeth that he couldn't dislodge.

The road made a turn ahead of them as it climbed the hill. He coasted into a stop and set the brake. They got out. As they moved to switch positions, Dawn pulled him down in front of the runner. She had a small pistol in her hand, which he hadn't seen before. A slug thrower.

"Three targets," she said. "Flanking us."

He couldn't see anything but didn't want to stick his head out for a better look. He readied his burner. In the darkness around them came the soft *tap-tap-tap* of metal feet on the sandy soil. The sound approached from both sides of the vehicle.

"You know how to use that weapon?" he whispered.

"Spent some time at the range."

"Then make your shots count."

Miles leaned out, leading with his burner, but didn't have a shot. The rocks around the side of the road might have all been spider bots. He shifted from target to target, unaccustomed to sighting using his real eye. Motion. He pivoted and fired but ducked as a red light flashed.

Dawn had crawled forward on the opposite side of the runner. Her weapon cracked twice. A spider lurched forward, but it was twitching. It pitched forward, legs propellering and spiked feet slashing the air. Miles scrambled to join her, saw a second shape scurrying up the road behind them, and snapped off a series of blasts. The bot wavered, and he shot it three more times until it went down. But a third drone appeared past the driver's side of the desert runner. Before he could move, Dawn stood, fired twice, and brought it down.

He was catching his breath as she swept the night with her pistol.

"Clear," she said.

"Are you sure?"

She delivered a coup de grâce to the bot before her and, with a final spasm, it lay still. Keeping low, Miles went to the other two and confirmed they were down, at least until some Metal Head collected them for recycling.

Dawn moved to the driver-side door. "Get in!"

But something about the third bot caught his attention. Its eye stalk bore a few newer parts which weren't made from the black steel or hadn't been painted. This was the one Hill had been working on. The hideout had three of the drones. All three were here now, disabled. And while the bots could see at night, he guessed not many of the gang could. There were no headlights in the desert.

They had a few minutes, at least.

"What are you doing?" she asked.

He climbed into the passenger seat. "Just a little math. Three bots in the hideout, three here. We might have bought ourselves some time, but it means the host is using the bots for something else."

He checked his burner before putting it aside next to the shifter. Two shots left. "You seem resourceful. Any chance you can fix my eye?"

She got the runner in gear and sped forward. "Maybe. Some light, some tools, and with no one shooting at us."

They drove up a few switchbacks to an intersection of trails marked by a white post. She slowed and then made a turn.

"Pretty good work with that pistol," Miles said.

Dawn dabbed sweat from her brow. "Thanks. Amazing what you can do when motivated."

"Hmm. 84 series? Post war, not many off the assembly matrix. Plus, you don't look that old. Not a mark on your skin. Classy stuff."

"What are you talking about?"

"Your modifications. 84 series. Or is there something newer than that in your skull?"

"I'm not a cyborg."

"Bull. Snap targeting. You hit those power plants dead on to knock them out like that. And I don't buy you happened to find that dead Metal Head and just happened to track me and the marshal out here by luck. It's night, it's dark, and you've got some kind of boosted night vision or infrared or both. Post-war Meridian tech can afford to make things look pretty. No glowing red eye. Just the goods, and no one's the wiser."

"I said I'm not—"

"Save it. My hearing in my augmented ear has never synched right with my brain, but with everything being as quiet as it is, I can hear the tiny noises when your eye focuses. Impossible to miss. So Herron-Cauley has a top-of-the-line combat model."

Dawn rolled her eyes. "Not combat. Just a few upgrades. Eyes. Computer interface module. Medulla governor, which helps with a steady hand."

"They don't do those anymore."

She smiled but her gaze remained hard and fixed on the road ahead. "How about you sit quietly? You've no doubt been through an ordeal. I'll get us to safety."

"This isn't the way to the train. Where are you going?"

"Seraph. It's what you wanted, isn't it? The passengers will be rescued by morning. The gang, the bots, they wouldn't attack the train. There's no point. This host you mentioned has you spooked."

"He believed it and was clear about what he was going to do," he said. "You can't just drive us away without us warning everyone."

She didn't answer.

He grabbed for the burner between the seats, but she was faster, snatching the weapon and aiming it at Miles' midsection. His left hand was his slow hand. Her right hand was wicked fast, steady, and he had no doubt she could put a hole in him before he could blink, if she wanted.

He said, "You've got two shots. Better make them count."

"If I wanted you dead, you'd be dead. Now shut up."

"You were packing your own weapon this whole time and never bothered to pull it when we were being attacked."

"We had you and the marshal to save us," she said plainly.

"You're not concerned about the train passengers. Just yourself. And me."

"You shouldn't have run. Meridian put a lot of money into you. Quarantining your software rights daemon was stupid. You would have been processed out. Why couldn't you wait?"

He chuckled. "Maybe you haven't done your homework. I've got last century's Insight module in my head. That doesn't just unplug. Meridian doesn't let its property walk, even if it's out of date. Why do you think I've been on active duty so long? They couldn't let me retire. They don't know what to do with me."

"Nonsense. There're good surgeons. I've seen them work. They even taught me a few tricks. But it doesn't matter now. Settle in. This road will take us south, and if we don't get delayed, we'll be in Seraph before morning. A rescue party will save the train. And you'll be returned to Meridian. They'll square you away."

Kill me, you mean. But he kept the comment to himself. She wasn't stupid, but was only telling him what any trained operator would say to a target you needed to keep under your control. Promise anything. Keep hope alive. It was when a mark knew they had no hope that they caused trouble.

He nodded at the burner pointing his direction. "Put that down before you put your eye out."

"It's not pointing at me."

"You've got two shots left. Doubt you missed that. There are more bad guys out here, and we'll need it."

The burner didn't waver.

Steering with one hand, she slowed to navigate a series of deep ruts. "You said it yourself. We took care of the machines that were chasing you. That's three more not attacking the train. The passengers will hold out. This host person is bluffing. And the flying drone which hit us? A big risk for anyone. If the people upstairs spot the launch site, they're dead."

The people upstairs. The watchers. Caretaker holdouts. Sore losers tucked away inside hollowed moon craters. Everyone knew why no one flew anywhere. Killer satellites in high orbit would shoot any plane or rocket down. But there hadn't been a recorded strike in thirty years. It didn't mean no one used an airplane, but they saved it for cloudy days.

He needed to push the matter and try another angle. "So when you're not lawyering, you do side work as a bounty hunter."

"Not to be rude, but why don't we both stay quiet and let me drive?"

"Turning your back on everyone at the train won't look good on your record. If the host follows through with his threat, they'll be murdered. We can do something about it."

"You're broken, and like you said, the burner has two shots. My pistol isn't the best weapon. So if the host has more toys, we can't stand against an army."

"Might not be an army, just a lot of parts that keep getting put back together. I didn't see any flying drone hardware in their hideout. And this host has kept himself separate from the gang. There must be another location in phone signal range. If I were to guess, it's the same place they took their prisoners."

She said, "I guess that's what they were trying to do with you just now. Capture you. If they wanted to kill you, they wouldn't have gotten so close. It's too risky and stupid. If they had decided to just burn you down, a one-eyed ex-cop with two charges in his flash gun wouldn't stop them."

He braced against the dash and ceiling as they jaunted over another rough section of road. "Now do you believe me when I say there's something out here that doesn't add up? Help me. You care. You know what a body blow it will be for Herron-Cauley if no one walks out of this alive. Maybe Meridian will be happy that Seraph will lose its luster, but that cat's out of the bag. Too many River City businesses are counting on trade, to Seraph, to New Pacific."

"That's too many mixed metaphors from a grunt like you."

"Will you pull over? Maybe we can't save the train if there's a wave of spider bots and Metal Heads about to attack them. At least we can still try to rescue the marshal. We might even pull the plug on this host and stop the whole thing from going down. It's a long shot, but consider the alternatives. All those people. You willing to have them on your conscience?"

"None of this is my fault," she said. "Us dying trying to track down where the marshal was taken does no one any good."

"I don't plan on dying."

"Sounds like you're set to go down in a blaze of glory. No thanks."

He looked out at the road ahead of them captured in the trapezoids of headlights, a drawbridge leading away from the train, the killer robots, and towards whatever fate Dawn's employers had in store. A blaze of glory? It wasn't what he wanted. He had started this journey by hiring the hacker who would free him from his technological shackles. It was supposed to end with leaving his son a nest egg, a last gesture which had eased his mind once he had set his plan into motion.

Now it was all slipping away from him.

But like so many of the choices he had made during moments of white-hot combat, when saving everyone wasn't possible, you save some.

Casually, as to not surprise Dawn, he rested his hand on the parking brake.

She pressed the burner against his ribs. "What are you doing?"

"We're stopping. This isn't up for debate. Fire if you have to. But I'm guessing Meridian wants me alive. Maybe the reason they want me is not the hardware but something I saw or did which is still lodged in my Insight module.

Doesn't matter. If you want to avoid a nasty roll, you'll get your foot off the accelerator."

"I'm warning you..."

"You know if you kill me, a lot of my mods won't do you any good. I hold the encryption, and it dies with me. Without it, it's mostly junk."

"Move your hand."

He kept it in place. Gripped the handle and prepared to pull. But before he could, she slowed them down and finally brought the runner to a stop.

"Look, Dawn, here's the deal. I'm going to try to bring the marshal home. You told me you saw no bots near the train. That will change soon. I have a feeling about this host. He didn't waste words. He has more than the spiders that were chasing me, and he may have assets I can't even begin to imagine. But I can't do it alone. You fix my eye. Give me the burner. You go back to the train and take charge and use your last few bullets to protect them. When this is over, I'll think about going with you."

"You'll think?"

"We're not there yet," he said.

"First, I'm not letting you go anywhere without me. We do this together. And even with your eye back online, the burner has two shots."

"You're forgetting about the runner's battery. Don't they teach you kids anything?"

Chapter Eighteen

The burner's battery recharge took less than five minutes. With the flip of a switch, this model of desert runner's engine became an industrial battery charger normally used on other vehicles. Miles spent the time crouched in the headlights and holding still while Dawn checked his cybernetic eye.

She held a small screwdriver from the runner's toolkit. "Not a burner wound. Targeting laser neutralized it, I'll guess."

A sensation of pressure, a click and pop, and she had his eye out.

"Minor damage to the lens. Probably should get that replaced later. Chip might be fried. Can't help that now with these tools. With the reset, you'll have limited targeting. Not sure how it will synch with your hand or your head."

"Will I be able to see?"

"Just a sec. Let's find out." She put the eye back in the socket. Sweat beaded on her forehead but her hands were steady.

"Nervous?"

She tightened the frame around the eye with a couple of precise movements. "I don't want to die out here, if that's the question."

"You'll be safer at the train."

"If your eye works, I'm not so certain. Unless you decide to try to take me out while we go chase the host. I'm going out on a limb here. We'd be safer driving south."

"You're doing the right thing."

She leaned away as if double-checking her work. He moved his eyes. At least it was connected to the muscles properly. Then the world appeared in his artificial right eye and synched with what he saw with his left. He focused on a rock at the edge of the field of illumination, then on Dawn's face. No targeting reticule appeared.

He said, "Software's off."

"Turn on your Insight."

"No. They might be able to track it. At least I can tell distance now."

He loaded the burner with the charged battery. Ten shots. He slid the weapon into the front of his belt and shook out his jacket before pulling it on.

She climbed into the driver's seat. The runner hummed to life. Her hand hovered over the shifter. "I can get us to Seraph. You'll have a chance to visit your boy before we go back to River City."

"I can't do that. And I'm hoping you can't either."

"All right. Then we head to this second hideout? And where is that, exactly?"

"Let's go to the bar first. There's someone there I hope will answer my questions and tell us where those bots take people."

***

Once downhill, Dawn switched off the headlights. The road beneath them was smooth. She made only minor steering adjustments, occasionally swerving past some unseen obstacle. Miles hung onto the loop handle above the passenger seat while gripping the burner. The fluttering in his stomach surprised him. Nerves. What had his old C.O. said? *"When the butterflies stop flapping, that's when you stop breathing. A case of nerves is your body's reminder that it wants to survive."*

He checked the charge again as if it might have changed in the last two minutes. Wiped dampness from his left hand on his slacks. With no aim assist, he'd have to rely on the weapon sights. He couldn't remember the last time he had been to a range. At least with a burner it was aim and shoot. Anything with bullets would have a kick, and then came the variables of ballistics. But the burner wasn't foolproof either, as a jerky trigger squeeze would still spoil his shot and atmospheric effects and reflective plating could weaken the impact. Fortunately, none of the walking drones they had encountered had much armor. He doubted Hill was the only mechanic the host had working on his machines. If what he had faced so far was all from recycled war surplus, then this host would become an even greater danger if he ever gained access to more materials.

"That the bar up ahead?" Dawn asked. The lights of the hamlet were out except for Zoon's place.

"Yes." Miles pointed to the end of the row of structures. "Go down the main drag. Slowly."

She eased up on their speed and rolled along the center street of the mining community. "No one home."

"Pull up in front of the bar."

He didn't wait for the runner to stop as he swung out of the cab and hurried for the broken window. Dawn was on his heels, her weapon poised and pointing at the ground, her head swiveling and checking behind them.

Mr. Zoon sat at a table and looked like a puppet whose strings had been cut. A device rested on the table in front of him. He didn't stir as Miles stepped through the shattered window and crunched on the glass.

Zoon jerked his head up as if he had been sleeping. His eyes went wide as Miles approached, and he grabbed for the device. Miles was faster. He snatched it up and took it to the bar where one of the glasses of water was waiting. He dropped it in.

Miles said, "This is going to be a conversation between us. No host. You and your daughter work for him. We're taking him down. You're either going to help me find him and everyone he's kidnapped, or it's not going to go well with either of you."

When Zoon didn't react, Miles kicked the table over.

"Tell me you understand."

"I don't know...I don't know where to find him. I'm not allowed to leave."

"No? Your daughter is out in that cave fixing his bots."

Zoon nodded. "She can come and go. Not me. Not me."

Dawn checked behind the bar and then vanished for a moment into the kitchen before returning. Mouthed, "All clear."

"Well, you've got to have a good idea about things, even if you're stuck here. The host took those people away from here, and it seems like it took a while. He's out in the desert, and I'm guessing in one of the mines. You deliver supplies and food to him using one of the delivery dogs?"

"Yes."

"How long does the dog take round trip?"

Zoon's face creased as he thought. "Hour and a half. Yeah, hour and a half every time."

Miles wanted to ask Insight how fast the average delivery bot walked over broken desert. But he could guess. He got out the miner's notebook. Three mines listed to guess from. But how many more might be out there?

"What direction do they go? You've watched them leave."

"East. Always east."

Twenty klicks. The notebook mentioned a hole east-northeast about that distance, and another just called the east hole, distance unknown. Neither a lock, and both were a long shot without knowing exactly how far the dog traveled, especially if the bots could be commanded to take a circuitous path or make more than one stop.

"There have to be fifty mines just within a hundred square kilometers of here," Dawn said. "The rail paid off more than a few of them to pack it up so the rail could be built. You tried, Miles. But we can't just go driving into the desert hoping we trip on the right one."

He hated that she was right. The desert was vast. The stories of folks flooding the wastes during the platinum rush had been circulating since he was a child.

Miles studied the barkeeper. "Is one of the dogs here, or do you wait for them?"

"They usually show up when there's an order. Sometimes they charge up here while I get things ready."

"Show me."

***

The small garage was easy to miss in the dark. In the building next to the bar, the delivery dog parking space was little more than a small hutch attached to the wall, which Miles had dismissed as a tool shed. But on closer examination, a power conduit was visible running from the roof. He hesitated only a moment before propping open the door.

A bot was folded inside. The small quadruped drone, a "delivery dog," was the size of a knee-high hound, with a battery, small brain, and space to attach cargo compartments for any variety of goods. This unit had a shoebox refrigerator attached, too small for meaningful food delivery. His examination confirmed a sealed interface. There was nothing to plug into, as the dog would receive its marching orders remotely. No brain to hack, so no way to learn its programming orders.

"Why does it have a cooler?" Dawn asked.

Zoon perked up, as if excited to share the answer. "Oooh! Ahh! Special deliveries! We get them sometimes from Seraph. I mind my own business. I mind it. But I read labels. And the dogs come and have me store medicines and pharmaceuticals. And then the host requests delivery."

Miles confirmed the small fridge set in the dog's body was empty. "What kind of drugs are we talking about?"

"That would be peeking, and the host would know."

"So the host only calls you. Let's say you receive a perishable shipment from Seraph you can't keep yourself and needs to be delivered. You have to have a way to tell this thing it has its order and it's time for it to make a drop-off."

Zoon began to stammer. Shook his head. Looked between Dawn and Miles as if they had both told him to perform contradictory tasks.

He swatted Miles and stumbled back. "No, no, no. He'll hurt us. He'll hurt us!"

"Take it easy. We're here. We're going to protect you."

"You can't."

Zoon was fumbling with something tucked in his belt. The marshal's hand cannon. He was bringing it up when Dawn fired. He let out a gasp and crumpled, the stubby gun dropping to the dirt. Miles kneeled next to him, but it was too late. Zoon was dead, the bullet having struck him in the heart. The echo of the gunshot died around them.

"I...could have disarmed him," Miles said.

She scooped up the hand cannon and patted Zoon down. "Maybe, maybe not. If they don't know we're here already, they do now. This is a dead end. You ruined his device, so that's out. We have to leave while we can. Are you listening?"

Miles forced his breathing to calm as he rose. He took off his hat and smoothed his hair back before setting the hat on his head. He considered the dog in the closet. A green charge light indicated its battery was full. He shut the power down in the closet and hit the manual release, which locked the dog in place.

Dawn watched the street and kept glancing his way. "What are you doing? Let's go."

He found a power switch on the dog. It had a reset toggle. He cycled the power down and watched as the indicator light vanished, only to pop up again.

The dog perked up, standing on all fours. It backed up to the charging closet as if to reconnect itself.

Miles nudged the metal creature back with his foot and closed the closet door. "Uh-uh. No more charging for you."

The dog took a moment, as if absorbing the news. Then it trotted into the street, paused, and began to run.

Miles ran too, with Dawn chasing after him. He crunched a knee against the dash as he climbed into the desert runner's driver seat. Dawn barely got in before he slid the shifter into gear and made a U-turn. Floored it. The delivery dog was nowhere in sight, but once he passed the last building and turned on the lights, he caught a glimpse of it.

Moment of truth. Would it head for Seraph, or go where it was supposed to deliver its medicine?

It was running east. He barely slowed as they bounded over a small embankment and followed.

Chapter Nineteen

It was Dawn's turn to cling for dear life. Miles navigated the desert runner past rocks and narrowly missed a sharp drop-off, which would have landed them in a narrow ravine, ending the nighttime mad pursuit of the delivery dog spectacularly.

"You think resetting that thing and sending it home is going to lead you to the marshal?" she asked. "How do you know the dog even belongs to this host? It could belong to a miner, a surveyor, or some merchant in Seraph. Or maybe it's broken and taking us to wherever it was manufactured."

Miles kept the dog in the desert runner's headlights. "It's heading east towards the mines."

"There are plenty of things further east, you know. Rivers, swamps, stretches of waste. Miles, are you listening?"

"Stop shouting. My ears work."

"All right, let's assume it belongs to the host and it's running home. You know this is a trap, right? If this host wants you, you're handing yourself over. This is stupid."

"I told you to go back to the train. Let me drive."

Wherever the dog was going, it wasn't trying to lose him. It sprinted at a steady clip, and the runner kept pace. But the dog threaded between boulder formations and bound over gaps which were show-stopping obstacles if Miles collided with them. Miles nearly lost his target a few times as he took necessary detours. But the dog's heading never wavered.

East, and slightly southward. Unless the dog made a turn, it ruled out J's mine from the notebook. That one was slightly north. It left the other two, one of which was marked to the east at an undetermined distance. All of this assumed the dog was heading to any of the locations listed.

Miles ignored the nagging thought that they should have returned to the train. Helped those stranded survive whatever attack was coming. But the marshal and the engineer were out there, and stopping the host might put this desert ghost and his handiworks out of business.

"Anyone on our tail?" Miles asked.

"I can't look. If I turn my head, I'm going to hurl."

The rearview mirror was missing. And if something was following them, it was running dark. He wished he could do the same, but then they'd lose the dog.

Acid roiled in his stomach. Zoon had pulled on them. But the man had lost his mind years ago. Miles could have talked him down. He tried to dismiss the thoughts, needed to focus. Dawn's words gnawed at him. Following the dog could take them anywhere. If the host was resourceful, there might be any number of remote charging stations. This would cost Miles hours and any chance of rescuing the marshal and the engineer would evaporate.

A darker thought manifested. He could strike a deal with Dawn. They could take the runner and finish the trip to Seraph and get what credits he could for his son in exchange for his life.

The dog vanished around a rocky slab. A wide channel led down between rising sandstone walls. The runner's headlights caught several piles of debris and a rusted hulk of what might have been an excavator. It leaned and was missing most of one of its tracks, a single long arm curling against its leaning body as if it had died a lonely death. The dog then became visible again as they coasted past the excavator. It walked slower now and moved towards a flat-roof shed. A series of solar panels occupied a portion of the canyon floor beyond.

A charging station. They had followed it to a charging station. Miles pulled up next to the shed. The dog pressed against a wall charger and plugged itself in. He got out and examined the bot. There were three other open charger receptacles. Excessive for such a remote operation, and three more than what he had found at Mr. Zoon's village.

Miles guessed the dogs would typically have enough juice for hundreds of kilometers of duty. A quick inspection confirmed the chargers were all functional. Yet everything appeared dusty and in need of cleaning. The solar panels, too. The accumulated grime would inhibit power collection and would eventually fail. Whatever mine was nearby was abandoned.

Dawn checked inside the shed. "There's nothing here."

He walked past the first rack of solar panels. Sections of canyon wall were scratched away, some with framing and covered entryways, but those were clotted with fallen rocks and tons of soil. No one was coming and going into the ground here.

"Miles?"

Several parked vehicles caught his eye. Also dusty, but not more than what he guessed was several weeks' worth of sediment. One was a larger desert runner, which seated eight and was equipped with pillowy tires for navigating soft terrain. It sat next to a bucket truck and an open-cab material handler with its pronged forks lowered to the ground. Unlike the excavator, all of these appeared to be in operating condition.

A check of the material handler's battery confirmed it. Charged up and ready to go.

Past the vehicles rose a heap of mine tailings which appeared darker than the surrounding earth, as if it retained moisture. He looked around some more. No tents, camping supplies, or signs of anyone living on site. Strange. Maybe in daylight he could search for footprints. He returned to the shed.

Dawn stood on their vehicle's running board. "There's nothing in there. Just an old water hole."

A capped well? He found the miner's notebook and flipped to the first entry for V, Y, and Company.

4 guards at capped well. No visual on primaries.

This was one of the mines the spy was watching. But why guard a well? The shack had a charging wall and, he discovered as he rounded the shed, a water gauge and standpipe and even a shower head. But the gauge showed no pressure.

He opened the door. The round stone circle rose a half-meter off the ground and had a plastic lid across the top. The lid slid away. A ladder descended into the well. On the roof of the shack was an electric winch he hadn't noticed before. The lid, the winch, the inside of the shack—none of it looked as dusty as anything else outside. In fact, a breeze struck his face. Cool air coming from below. Ventilation. This was no abandoned mine. But it also had no visible guards.

Dawn rushed to the cover of the shack and crouched, her pistol out, her eyes wide. "Company."

Miles did a combat peek. At the edges of the reflected headlights, a large black shape that wasn't there before blocked the way out of the mining camp.

He pulled the burner. "It's bigger than any of the drones. What is that thing?"

"It's a drone, all right. Not as fast as the others, but definitely heavy duty."

"Maybe it's a mining machine. I'm going to take a shot."

"Miles, don't—"

He leaned out and snapped off a laser round, hitting the machine dead center. Besides a brief flash at the point of impact, the drone didn't respond. Miles kept watching as the bot moved a moment later. Four articulated fingers rose, barely noticeable. Dawn tugged on him as a distinct whine ramped up. They tumbled into the shack and hit the floor as a series of burner blasts perforated the walls. Sparks flew from an electric panel.

A heavy *thump-thump-thump* grew closer from outside.

Miles rose on to his knees and peered into the well. "It's coming. Down the hole."

Dawn didn't argue. She scrambled over the lip and climbed quickly. Miles put his weapon away and followed as the door to the shed tore open.

"Faster, faster, faster," he murmured, both to Dawn and to his own hands and legs.

He climbed quickly, not taking the time to confirm the safety of each foot and handhold. Meanwhile, the shed above him was being torn to pieces.

Dawn was at the bottommost rungs and dropped, tucking and rolling out of sight.

A dark shape eclipsed the scant illumination above them. The massive drone whirred and clicked as it mounted the top of the well. Armored plating protected each limb. Once it brought its suite of lasers to bear, it wouldn't miss.

He swung down to the last rung and let go, landing on stone and crawling to get out of the drone's sight. It let out an electric buzz, as if perturbed by his not presenting himself as a target.

Rows of overhead lights set into the ceiling flickered on. The space below the well was a small chamber with support columns. Lockers and storage racks lined two walls, and three tunnels went off into the earth. Power conduits descended from the well and branched out along the ceiling. A water line, too. The place looked clean and the plumbing new.

Miles strained his ears. The big drone didn't seem to be going anywhere.

Dawn rifled through a hanging rack of mining overalls. "Maybe it can't get down here. But let's not wait to find out."

He considered blasting at the thing's underside but didn't want to waste his burner charges. "No shot. It's armored and we'll need something bigger than a hand burner. That thing's guarding the entrance like it doesn't want us to leave."

Among the equipment were headlamps. They each took one. With better light, Miles realized the floor of the mine chamber told a story. Tiny dimples in the dust spoke to the hundreds of drone feet which had passed through, heading to or from each of the three corridors. More disturbing were the drag marks. A few dark speckles were either oil or blood. These led to the center passageway. The water line running along the ceiling made a soft hiss as the liquid inside churned through the pipe.

The host's voice echoed from unseen speakers. "Is that you, Miles Kim? I thought we had an arrangement. A pity, but all is not lost. Because now that you're here, I have a new use for you and your companion."

Miles and Dawn eased their way down the center shaft. The floor at their feet was amazingly clean and free of debris.

"If you would be so kind," the host said, "do me the courtesy and put your weapons away." But the speakers must have been in the entry chamber, as the voice was behind them now.

They walked quietly, neither speaking. For someone who was supposed to be a lawyer, Dawn kept her weapon moving, sweeping the corridor behind them and following Miles' every move. But there was only one way to go. The shaft grew wider, the walls, ceiling, and floor smoother, with support braces free of any signs of wear or corrosion. The passage made a few turns. At each were other corridors which were filled with earth and stone, as if having suffered cave-ins.

Patches of minerals along the walls glittered. Miles could only wonder what had been mined there. Was there still gold or platinum to be had? And where were the miners? He was breathing too fast. His chest grew tight. None of this made any sense except for desert madness, but the bots, the town, the gang, and the robbery all spoke of design and intelligence.

A sharp smell stung his nose. Something medicinal, or an industrial strength disinfectant.

They stepped onto a grating. No moisture on the ground past this point. Air blew down around them. Miles' first instinct was to jump back, but instead he moved forward towards a steel door with a plastic curtain hanging across it.

A camera mounted above the doorframe whirred. "This is as far as you go with your weapons," the host said. "Place them on the floor before proceeding."

From the shaft behind them came the steady thuds and whirrs of a bot heading in their direction, and it sounded big.

Chapter Twenty

Miles braced himself on the corner and took aim down the corridor in the direction of the oncoming sounds. "Can you open that door?"

Dawn made a quick examination of the front of the vault. "There's no control panel or switch. Must be remote only."

"Figure something out."

They were trapped in a dead end, and the big bot was coming for them. As it came into view, Miles confirmed it was the same or identical to the one outside by the well. It was hunched down on all its legs, as the ceiling was too low. But the restricted space wasn't stopping it from creeping towards them like a giant black beetle. It scraped the ceiling and crushed a set of lights.

Miles tried to spot any weakness in the armor plating. "Anything?"

"Yeah, if I had an hour and a tool kit."

He shot the bot. The laser blast burned a bright cherry on the armor, which faded instantly. The bot paused to free a foot, which had caught on a bulge in the stone. One of its weapon fingers popped up and pivoted to aim.

Exhaling to steady his hand, Miles fired again. The bot's finger sizzled and drooped. But the machine freed itself and began crawling faster towards them. In a moment, it wouldn't need to shoot them down, as it could just as easily crush them in the enclosed space of the mine. And the bot had more weapons. The armored plates shifted as additional fingers with burners emerged.

Miles snapped off two more blasts before ducking. But this time he had aimed for the forward feet. The bot made a screeching sound, metal against stone. Dawn took cover next to him as the bot peppered the steel doorway with a triplet of laser bursts.

"Miles Kim," the host said. "please stop. This violence is pointless. You won't be harmed."

"Call off your machine!"

"This is futile. I don't want to hurt either of you. You both have value to me."

"Give me your gun," Miles whispered.

She handed the weapon over without question. With her pistol in his left hand and the burner in his right, he gave himself a three count. The bot kept scraping forward. A solid *thump* sounded like the machine striking the ceiling. It was moving and off balance, but it wouldn't be long before it made the corner.

Miles popped out and emptied Dawn's pistol into the bot while raising the burner and firing at the bot's weapon fingers. The bot flinched as it was struck. He got six shots off but didn't pause to see how many hits. He tumbled forward, dropping the pistol while gripping the burner. At the opposite corner now, he caught his breath and ignored all his training and instincts, which reprimanded him: *you don't break from perfectly good cover unless you want to die.*

Dawn reached for the dropped pistol. A laser blast made her flinch. The bot still had at least one of its weapons able. Miles peeked. The single laser finger pointed at him and a burner shot singed the air as he ducked back.

Once again, one shot left.

At the opposite corner, Dawn waved something at him. A magazine for her pistol. But bullets appeared to have done little to the giant machine.

He pointed at her and then her gun on the ground before motioning with his own. She nodded as if the exchange made sense. It didn't. Distracting the bot with his final shot so she could arm herself would be a futile gesture and would only delay the inevitable or get them both killed.

This was the time for sensible surrender. They couldn't know for sure what the host intended. And while it couldn't be good, every moment not dead meant they had a chance at getting away. But with so many missing miners, and everything they had witnessed, the host wasn't being gentle with whatever his plans were. He had proven himself a murderer and would say anything to get them to give up. The question which continued to nag him was why did the host want him alive so badly?

Dawn moved, and now it was Miles who hesitated.

When Dawn grabbed again for the pistol, the bot had been ready. A laser shot struck her arm and she screamed and fell to the floor. Miles emerged, sighted the last of the bot's weapon fingers, and fired, sheering the digit clean off. But the bot surged forward, driven up by its remaining four legs and oblivious to the two damaged forelimbs which plowed furrows and scraped the grating.

Stepping over Dawn, Miles took her pistol and the magazine, fumbling for a split second as he nearly dropped both. The bot barreled towards him. Dawn scrambled for cover. Miles got the weapon loaded and jumped for the machine.

He shoved his metal arm between a gap in the armor plates. Even as the bot cinched its body up, trapping him, he opened fire until the pistol clicked empty.

Something in the bot hissed and sent up a jet of compressed gas and hydraulic fluid. The machine sagged.

Miles tugged, but couldn't get his arm free. "A little help."

Dawn was behind him, but was busying herself with something. The smell of burned hair and skin struck his nose. She was winding a purple scarf around her right forearm. The limb trembled and she winced as she tugged the makeshift dressing tight.

"There're tools back here," she said. "Just a sec."

She vanished out of sight. Scraping sounds and something was being bent. She returned moments later carrying a two-handed pick. With her uninjured arm, she took a moment to wedge the narrow side of the pick head between the plates pinning him. But the two pieces separated with minimal effort, no doubt helped along with the lack of hydraulic pressure.

Miles slipped free. He rolled his shoulder a couple of times before inspecting the bot. Found the destroyed power plant. The bot was dead and down, and they could squeeze past and head out. He scooped up his dropped burner. The battery was dead. He slipped it into his belt.

"You okay?" he asked.

"It's burned down to the bone. I have pain management tools, but I'm not sure if they're working. Let's not stand around."

Miles moved to the vault door. "Open up now, or we break it down."

Was the host listening? To his surprise, the door emitted a deep hum before swinging open.

Miles had seen many horrors during the last act of the war and plenty of crime scenes during his work as a military cop. But nothing prepared him for this.

A dozen large metal tubes lined both walls of a long vault. They were fed by pipes and had machines attached, which churned and whispered. Each tube had a blank monitor and a window and was large enough to house a person.

He recognized the containers. They were old model auto docs, the kind used on spacecraft to assist with surgery. They were also used to control an occupant's metabolism, sending them into a torpor state to make long space flights. None of the colony missions had used them after it was shown that humans didn't recover from this kind of long sleep. Thus the nickname: coffins. That kind of hibernation had been abandoned in favor of long-lived volunteers who would parent the next generation of exoplanet settlers.

As the lights flickered to life above them, he could make out what was inside each coffin.

A person.

An operating room stood to the left. The sterilizing scent was stronger. A bin at the foot of a steel table was full of discarded bloody dressings. Bulbous vessels attached to the plumbing bubbled. And at the far side of the room, a terminal stood at the center of a network of bundled cables which ran from each of the beds.

Miles walked forward across puddles of liquid. Found the chief engineer. Found the marshal. Their eyes were closed, and they were suspended in a bluish fluid. They had masks on their faces and their hair had been shaved. The others? No doubt the missing miners. And who else might also be among those preserved here?

White frost lined Miles' breath as he spoke. "What is this?"

"Treasure," the host's voice said. "They come to the desert in search of it while each, in turn, holds something far more precious than platinum."

"I don't understand."

"Expertise. Knowledge. Memories. Things that would fade over time, I preserve alive for the ages. And with each offering, my pool of shared wisdom grows. With the train engineer, I can finish my work on my greatest achievement and start building my reactor. With the marshal, I have a bank of knowledge detailing the workings of Seraph business and politics. You could have been my agent there. Alas, now I have another purpose for you."

"Sealed up in a stasis pod? No thanks."

The host sighed. "A principled person would understand. They're hard to come by out here. My work was always as a provider before this. I *cared* for people. Saw to their every need. I could procure anything for my customers when things were scarce. Perhaps you remember those times."

Miles nodded at the rows of metal stasis pods. "Explain them. That's caring for people?"

"It used to be necessities which I procured. Then came luxuries. But when the settlers realized the desert was to be their permanent home, their needs became more acute. They required medicine, communication, technology and its machinery, food, and transportation. An infrastructure rose which bypassed my modest network. The thriving communities and their satellites grew once these were provided. I had to reinvent myself to remain relevant. What this infrastructure lacked was information. This deficiency was crippling for a nascent community straddling two city states set at each other's throat. But information became my new commodity."

Miles clenched his jaw. "That doesn't explain locking these people in these tanks."

Dawn kept her injured arm cradled. She eased her way towards the computer nexus at the end of the room. Examined the terminal.

"The desert would always subsist at the mercy of Meridian or New Pacific. But what if it became essential to both? A brokerage house for data and a hub for all information? Secrets for sale to the highest bidder? Mind you, I had competition in my new endeavor, but after a failed assassination attempt, I realized my new potential."

"What secrets?" Miles asked. "How does hooking these people up like this accomplish any of that?"

"Proof of concept, of course. Can a man take what another knows and make it their own? Start with the skills of a miner. It's what I did. Some of these have studied engineering and geology and metallurgy and are masters in their field who came here to put their knowledge to the test by working the ground. What they know is now mine. Now I can single-handedly operate any remote machine with the confidence of a dozen experienced prospectors, comprehend the clues that would tell me where to start drilling, understand how to do all this without excessive waste or pollution."

"He's reading their minds," Dawn said.

"No. No cursory-level brainwave pattern interpretations via magnetic resonance imaging or electroencephalogram. I'm talking about memories, deepseated knowledge, skills, and the wisdom which comes from a lifetime of experience."

Dawn was shaking her head. "A ripper, then. It's nothing new. It's banned tech made illegal before anyone ever even thought about leaving Earth to live someplace else."

"Nothing so crude. Their brains and central nervous systems are intact, only their consciousnesses are now in synch with mine. Now imagine a network of a hundred minds, a thousand, each node bringing a lifetime of expertise and skills."

"These are people, not volunteers," Miles said.

"Who will be restored once I'm finished with my experiment."

"This is monstrous. This experiment ends now."

The host's tone took an edge. "Damaging or turning off any of my equipment will only succeed at killing the subjects. They're in no pain. Even the most unskilled drudge contributes to the network's processing power. And each node becomes a receptacle of the other node's skills. In a word, they all learn what the other knows. Now if the two of you would please step outside the vault, we can discuss our options."

A red eye above the metal doorway flashed to life, watching them.

Miles made a quick examination of the marshal's tank. Locking T-bolts held the lid in place. He placed his hand on one, but hesitated. If the host was telling the truth, opening it would kill the marshal. He began walking from tank to tank. Was one of them the host?

"Mr. Kim, Ms. Moriti?" the host called. "Time for you to leave."

Dawn crouched and began working at a battery connected to the terminal.

"What are you doing?" Miles asked.

She didn't look up. "Ending this."

He pulled her away from the computer. "You can't risk killing everyone."

"They're already dead. There's no coming back from getting your mind plugged into a ripper. Let go of me—"

She screamed. An electric jolt ran through Miles' hands, which sent him to the floor. All his muscles tightened. Dawn doubled over and collapsed against one of the tanks. A pint-sized spider bot scurried over her. It raised an arm, which crackled and sparked. It had just shocked her and the electric charge had run through her and into him, nearly knocking him unconscious. She lay limp. He fought to get his own limbs moving, kicking feebly at the bot as it scuttered across her legs towards him.

It delivered a crackling stab to his foot. The spark popped as it discharged against the heel of his boot. He caught it with a foot, knocking it aside, but it bounced once and regained its balance. Moving quicker, it bounded towards him.

He pulled the burner out from his belt. Swung. His weak blow barely fazed the thing. A sharp jolt made him drop his weapon. He continued to back away. The room had nothing he could pick up. He pulled his jacket off and threw it over the spider. Even as it tore the fabric and lashed out with its prod, he leaped over it. A small door in the operating area, which he hadn't noticed before stood open. He raced for it and pulled it shut. The bot bounced against the door with a thud a second later.

He was inside a closet or storeroom. There was no latch and no lock on the handle. Then an electric surge zapped his hand through the doorhandle, sending pain lancing up through his arm and shoulder. He faltered, but kicked at the door as it began to open. He found a mop pole and braced it against the door frame. It stood a few centimeters open.

The drone's feet grabbed at the edges of the door. Miles knew the moment he let go it would be able to squeeze through.

"Mr. Kim?" the host called from outside. "While I had hoped our arrangement might include your cooperation, I would see your life spared, and that of Ms. Moriti. Our kind must look after one another. And it's those who made us who will now serve."

Miles' throat was too dry to swallow. His arms were numb, and he felt the door slipping. The host was talking about people without cybernetic enhancements. With a cold chill, he realized this was the crux of the host's actions. None of the faces he had seen appeared to have any kind of external implants.

One of the drone's talons reached through the gap in the door and slashed at him.

He grabbed it and tried to break it, but the limb slipped out of his grip and sliced his hand open.

A heavy-duty folding table stood against one of the walls. He gave himself a three count and grabbed it, slamming the bot as it tried to squeeze into the closet. Miles pressed himself against the table. The drone smashed against it before stabbing small holes into the dense material. Several zaps followed, but the table only conducted the smallest portion of the electric charges.

It still hurt.

"Mr. Kim, stop this. Everything you've fought for, you deserve. What Meridian took, they can never replace. The modifications they gave us weren't gifts but leashes to keep their soldiers in line. You can have the life you wanted, free from any master. That's what I fight for. Don't let misplaced compassion blind you to the truth that it's their turn to pay."

Another drone arm reached through, and then a second on the other side of the table. Were there two of the bots now trying to push their way in? More?

Miles' voice cracked as he was out of breath. "Make up your mind, will you? Are you fighting a war or building something? This us versus them idea falls apart pretty quickly. Who gets to be on your team? Someone with a bionic limb? A replaced hip? Braces?"

"I tire of this, Mr. Kim. My patience is at an end. I need ones who will fight by my side and share my dream and the profits. If you stand against me, then so be it. I will mourn for you."

New skittering sounds across the floor outside of the closet. Miles couldn't guess how many bots were coming, but they'd overwhelm him.

He was sunk. They had him. He had failed in the simple task of making it to Seraph and cashing in on the only thing he owned. Dillan would survive and maybe prosper, but he would never know about his father's attempt to provide one last financial boost and a goodbye note, which Miles had never completed.

His arms ached from the strain. The tingling in his shoulder and hands only grew worse as he pressed his head against the table. From the sound of metal scratching on metal, the drones were climbing over each other. A claw swiped at him from above. Miles readied himself and with a final push heaved the table forward while backpedaling. The cramped closet had enough space that he could take a few steps towards the rear wall before having no place left to go.

The table bumped and turned as the bots swarmed over and around it. They paused as the last of them freed themselves from beneath the table.

As he grabbed the wall and prepared for the final rush, his hand touched an electrical conduit which fed into a large junction box. Like so much of the newer construction inside the mine, it appeared to have been done recently and quickly. It only had a few anchors holding it to the wall.

A futile gesture, he knew, and the possibility of electrocuting himself would only add a sadder note to these last moments.

He grabbed the conduit with both hands, braced his feet, and pulled as hard as he could.

Chapter Twenty-One

With a sharp pop, the lights went out.

Miles released the conduit and backed into the corner, unsure whether the line was hot or if the host or miners or whatever bot had laid the electrical work had bothered with breakers. While he wasn't particularly handy, he knew when to hire professionals.

From the sound of it, the drones were edging their way forward. Did these have any kind of night vision or light amplification? Surely so far down in the mine, they still wouldn't be able to see much. Infrared, on the other hand, meant they'd spot him as easily as if he were standing in a beam of sunlight.

The walls had brackets mounted in them. Using these as handholds, he pulled himself up and planted a foot on the junction box. His arms were already shaking, but now his legs trembled. He focused and fought to concentrate.

The bots' feet clicked across the floor as they advanced. And now they were milling about, bumping into one another and the walls.

They're blind.

He fought to quiet his breathing and was afraid they'd hear his thumping heart.

The loose conduit flashed a massive spark as one of the bots touched it. The machine squealed and tumbled and thrashed about. The other spiders began to scurry around faster like confused insects.

Miles' hands were slick. He began slipping. It would only take one of the creatures to stun him and it would be over. And the host must have a backup system for light and a way to repair damage like the dislodged power box.

A few more sparks blossomed. While no more bots received shocks, the flashes outlined the closet and the doorway. Too far to make it in one jump. The best Miles could hope for was to leap and run for it. So many shadows milled about near his feet. How they had missed seeing him was beyond him, but the sparks were leaving retinal burn-in on his artificial eye, so maybe the spiders only possessed rudimentary visual sensors that were likewise hampered.

He'd slip if he waited any longer. He sprang towards the door, his legs instantly seizing up in a cramp which sent him sprawling. He didn't wait to see what he landed on. At least one bot squirmed beneath him. He leaped haphazardly forward through the door and slammed it shut with both feet. Several spiders bounced off the door, but they were trapped inside the closet, and now Miles could hold the door shut.

An emergency light from the coffin room reflected enough illumination, which outlined the operating theater. Miles rose and grabbed for a steel table and heaved it against the door. More thuds, but the little buggers were trapped for the moment. He paused to catch his breath, scanning the floor for any more of the things.

Stacks of crates stood against a wall next to the cabinets. He caught a few labels. The scan codes he couldn't read, but the tags had item descriptions. Medical equipment, medicine, and chemical supplies, and so much of it. Some of what he saw had shipping stickers and tracking labels. Did the host purchase what he needed?

Something to file for later.

Dawn lay unresponsive where she had fallen. Still had a pulse, still breathing, but she didn't stir when he gently patted her cheek.

A few lights pulsed on the terminal and each of the tanks, but otherwise it appeared as if his pulling the conduit had only blacked the room out. Battery backup, no doubt, and the host was probably scrambling to send more machines to repair what Miles had broken.

One of the coffins next to the terminal began to churn. Miles stepped back as bubbles percolated. The entire tank lit up along with a keypad and display. The door hissed, and a cloying, rotting aroma filled the air.

The man who stepped out of the tank was covered in plastic. He began to peel it away, uncovering prosthetic arms and legs and most of his head and neck. There was more metal and plastic than flesh. He was impossibly thin, a skeleton walking. The portions of remaining skin had red moles and dark blemishes and other spots, but the tissue itself was so pale it was almost translucent. Portions of his cheeks and throat were taut and pinched by the steel grafts and appeared as if they might tear. Finally, he stripped off the mask. Attached was a tube which ran into his throat, and this too came out and dropped to the floor, spilling more of the liquid at his feet.

He began to breathe deeply, his chest heaving. His cloudy eyes looked about and blinked a few times before his attention fixed on Miles.

"You...you fool."

On the floor near him, Dawn regained consciousness. Her arms and legs appeared to not be cooperating as she inched away from the man. Her eyes were wide, and she kept trying to speak, but no words were coming out.

The host coughed and spat out a string of saliva. "You've made things difficult, Miles Kim."

"I'm sorry to have inconvenienced you."

"My machines have work to do. The tanks will operate off battery reserves. You've accomplished nothing. You've wasted your effort in this."

"And you're leaking."

Between the host's sagging belly skin and the metal chassis which formed his pelvis, a darker liquid had begun dribbling, tracing lines down the sinews of his thighs.

"More repairs," the host said, as if discovering a door which wouldn't close properly or a hinge which needed a dab of oil. "You could have provided a service. I need to procure another doctor. More battery backups as well. You could have tasted what I have, the memories of all these ones, lifetimes, and experiences. But there are others who understand. Those that won't, those like you, must step aside. Alas."

Miles backed up far enough so he could see the closet. While the bots continued to bang against the door, the table remained in place. But from outside the vault came the metal-on-stone footsteps of more incoming drones, along with flashes of brilliant illumination. These bots were equipped with lights.

There was no other way out. Miles realized with a dark certainty the only course left. He grabbed the vault door. The automatic hinges whined as he pulled, but without power, they didn't stop him from swinging the door shut.

"What are you doing?" the host asked.

"Locking us in here."

The inside of the door had several bars which needed power to lock, but using his full weight, he managed to pull a heavy latch closed. A moment later, something tapped at the door.

The host began to limp his direction. "Get away from there."

Dawn grabbed one of his legs with both arms, sending the host to the floor. He kicked and swatted at her, knocking her away. Miles recovered his spent burner and rushed over. With a meaty thud, he clobbered the host across the head.

"Uhnh! You...you can't..."

He helped Dawn up and moved her away from him. "Let's get these other tanks open."

"No!" the host screamed. He got up, his legs shaking.

"You revived well enough without any extra help. This might be the only chance we get before something breaks in here and stops us."

The tapping outside continued without letup.

Dawn gave him an are-you-sure look, but moved to the first of the tanks near the vault door. Liquid drained out. A shriveled gray husk dangled from a series of tubes.

She examined the suspended figure before stepping back to appraise him. "He's dead."

The host struggled to rise but stopped when Miles raised the burner as if to strike him again.

Dawn went to the next coffin, but now spent a moment with the touch screen. "This one's also gone. The next one too." Down the line she went until she came to the chief engineer. "Monitor shows a heartbeat. He's breathing."

"Without power, they will all perish," the host said. "Let me save them. Get me to my tank."

Miles shot him a warning finger. "Move, and I knock you down again. Insight, wake up."

Now it didn't matter if the host and his drones were hunting him using the ambient signals from his device.

Across his eye, lines of gibberish scrolled, which told him the computer attached to his brain was cycling through its reboot. He crouched to examine the engineer's tank. Spotted a serial number plate. Off-Earth manufacturer. All he needed was a summation of a user guide. Insight rewarded him with a barrage of information from its memory, with so many warnings and cautions and safety instructions for any installer that it took a moment to digest it all. At least it was in English.

Directions for wiring, bonding, maintenance, and setup scrolled past.

Under "Authorized Users Must Be Medical Professionals!" he found the troubleshooting menu.

Insight began to read to him, *"Emergency patient retrieval may result in cardiac arrest, seizures, and drowning!"*

"Shut up, Insight," Miles said. "Summary: patient retrieval protocol."

"*Select terminate hibernation sequence from operator's menu. Confirm automation sequence and enter authorization code.*"

"There's an authorization code?"

Dawn tapped at the touch screen. "Not on any of these."

"Then get him out. Get all of them out."

She didn't hesitate, but went to work. Using the tank software resulted in the fluid draining off before the door opened. The engineer sagged. Miles' heart sank. But then Dawn began to disconnect him. His eyes popped wide open. He coughed weakly as Miles helped get him free of the clear mask and breathing tube. Miles assisted him out of the coffin and leaned him on the step at the base of the tank.

The bots at both the vault door and closet continued to make a racket without letup.

The marshal was next. Dawn sent the tank through its emptying cycle. The big man thrashed and clawed at Miles as the mask and tube in his throat were removed. But then he went limp. Miles almost dropped him as he eased him to the floor. The operating room's supplies had sheets and wrapped bundles of bandages. Miles did his best with these to make the marshal comfortable.

Dawn went to the rest of the tanks. "Three more are still alive, but they have weak life signs."

"Then leave them until we can get help."

The host drooped. His head was propped against a wall as the rest of his body lay limp. "Help me to my tank. I can help them. I can help all of them."

"Most of your victims are already dead."

"No. No, they're part of me. They'll be immortal with me. We will live forever."

When the host tried to push himself up, he slid back down to the floor. A series of convulsions ran through his body. His chest rose and fell in a series of moist gasps. He tried a few times to reach for something that wasn't there. Miles took his hand, metal fingers meshing with metal fingers.

"I can't die," the host whispered.

Miles hated to contradict him.

Chapter Twenty-Two

Miles left the host where he lay and checked on the marshal. Barma had multiple cuts on his face, and the fingers on his left hand were mangled. Bone showed from one of the joints. Whatever surgery had done to get him ready for hibernation didn't include the hand, and the marshal wouldn't let Miles touch it.

The marshal's voice was thick with phlegm. "Never mind that. How bad's my face?"

"You'll give me a run for my money. But you'll heal."

"And what about him? The host?"

"He's gone."

"If you find any pain meds, set me up. Whatever he gave me is fading."

The bots in the closet kept tapping, but Miles felt a growing confidence that the tiny drones didn't have the strength or guile to figure out how to escape. Miles made a more thorough search of the operating room and its storage cabinets. Discovered it was well-stocked and organized with even more packaged supplies. All of it appeared new, as if a shipment from a Meridian hospital had been dropped off and signed for.

With Insight's help, he selected a self-contained dose of painkiller and administered it to the marshal. The man nodded his thanks, leaned back against his makeshift pillow, and closed his eyes.

"You want one for your arm?" Miles asked Dawn.

She had been crouching next to the host's tank for several minutes, working at his keypad. "I'll be fine. Looks like I've got radio. At least as long as the battery power works."

"How about shutting down his network and his killer robots?"

"That's encrypted. But the communications aren't. I've got a message looping for anyone who might hear us."

"What's the range?"

She scrolled down on the touchscreen. "Can't tell. Might not be anything, which means we're stuck."

"Keep trying," he said. "Keep listening."

"Like there's anything else to do. Is that vault door going to hold?"

"Not if more heavy machinery shows up," he said. "It's only metal, and some of those mining bots have plasma cutters."

"Your Insight module tell you that, Miles?"

"There's a reason I shut it up as often as I do."

Miles went to check on the engineer. The man had passed out as he leaned on his open coffin, his breathing shallow. While the vault felt like it had air, with the power out, Miles couldn't help but worry that the ventilation system might also shut down. He decided not to ask Insight how long they could survive on the oxygen contained within the enclosed space.

Then a thought crossed his mind. "What about the delivery dog?"

"What about it?"

"It's not part of the mining network, is it?"

"No, they typically are on open bandwidths so they can be located and given directions in case of problems. The ones in Seraph are all part of a business co-op which funds them, since everyone uses them."

"So we can send a message using it."

"Assuming it didn't get destroyed by that mining bot which was chasing us."

"Do you have its frequency? Can you call it? Because if the host used it..."

She didn't wait to answer as she searched the screen. "Got it. It's here. Sending it to Seraph will take about eight hours, according to the delivery estimate. We won't last that long."

"Look for a history log of charge nodes. There are other communities out in the desert. The host might have bought or traded for some of the stuff down here from someplace nearby. If he wasn't robbing trains, he has to have some means of working with suppliers. And if not him, then the miners did. Why else would he keep using the dogs, if not for convenience?"

"There's one close by. A camp called The Gift Which was the Clean Spring."

"Somebody's going to have to explain these place names to me. Can you send the camp a message and get the dog to deliver it?"

"Simple enough." She started typing.

While Miles was curious what kind of call for help she was composing, he didn't want to delay what might be their last shred of hope in seeing daylight again.

She leaned back from the screen. "There. It's off. Now we wait to see if anyone wants to save us."

"You don't sound hopeful."

"People come to the desert to mind their own business. And with gangs like the Metal Heads roaming around, why would anyone bother to respond? The nearest train substations could be the only ones who might hear us. But they're—"

She didn't finish the thought. She didn't have to.

The bleak land beyond Meridian was as cold as the place which had spawned it. But then he thought of Dillan, who had known the names of just about everyone in their twenty-unit housing block, had fetched groceries for old Mrs. Moore for three years before her death, would spend an hour trying to track down the owner of a dropped wallet without an ID, and helped out on the hottest afternoons in the community garden even before he learned to like vegetables. Folks like Dillan had come to Seraph and the desert. Miles could only hope others had, too.

He checked on the closet and confirmed none of the bots were getting out, as a sudden silence told him they had stopped beating themselves against the door. But something big was moving outside the vault. The vibrations began in the floor, but soon shook the walls and ceiling above. Heavy machinery was inbound, but at least they'd have to clear the dead bot first.

Dawn appeared lost in thought and wouldn't make eye contact as Miles paced. The marshal shivered. Miles found his discarded torn jacket and added it to the sheets covering the marshal. Then he checked the touch screen on the host's stasis tube. The message programs were running, but a red flashing bar indicated a request to connect the network to power.

Once the power was out, the message for help would stop. They had enough emergency lights, at least. There were no other doors, and even if they could get into the closet, it would make for a poor last stand.

He nudged Dawn. "You should get into the tube. The bots will miss you when they break in."

She shook her head. "Claustrophobic."

"I'm serious. Those machines aren't going to play nice."

"And I'm serious too. My palms started sweating just thinking about it. If this is it, then this is it. We did our job."

"Did we?" he asked.

"The host was clearly delusional. And now he's out of the picture. I believe the people on the train get to see the sun rise. If it's any consolation, Herron-Cauley has some deep pockets."

Miles had his doubts, but he kept them to himself. Too many what-ifs about what the bots in the desert and the gang might be up to.

A shuddering squeal of metal-on-metal cut through the vault.

Miles got up and got under one of the marshal's arms. "Help me with him."

The marshal murmured a protest as they brought him to the host's tank and got him reclined.

"We close it up just enough. The bots miss him. At least one of us tells the story of what happened."

But the marshal swung a leg out of the tank and began pushing himself upright. Miles tried to stop him when a hard clang reverberated from the vault door. Then silence. Then the lights flickered, and the tank's screen went dark.

Chapter Twenty-Three

Hours passed, and no more noises came from outside the vault. The emergency light was their sole source of illumination. Except for the marshal's labored breathing and the occasional liquid murmur from the powered-down tanks, the silence was complete and stifling.

The marshal sat leaning against the host's coffin with Miles' jacket wrapped around him. His face was sullen. Any time Miles tried to ask how he was doing, the marshal waved him off with his uninjured hand.

Dawn kept worrying the fringe of her dress while chewing her lip. She sat across from the marshal and appeared lost in thought. She had spent about thirty minutes tinkering with the dead tank control panel and had gotten into the master terminal's guts, only to give up. Disconnected memory chips and other computer peripherals were stacked in a small pile.

"Find anything useful?" Miles asked.

"Just junk. Some of this is old, old, old, and it's locked me out."

Miles put an ear to the vault door. Whatever machines had been making a racket were now quiet. Were they waiting for orders, or pausing before their final assault? Miles knew he was being irrational, but grew concerned that even the sound of his breathing might trigger their attack, as if the machines were savvy hunters only looking for a confirmation their prey was still there.

No, he reminded himself, they were drones following orders. And with the host dead, they were on autopilot. He considered the handle to the door. They'd have to check outside eventually if no one came, if even just to let in more air. He decided he'd go, but for the moment he'd wait.

He paced some more and considered the engineer. The man now lay on the metal surgical table, which was still set against the closet door. He had grown catatonic and unresponsive. His heart? Some drug the host had given him? Insight was no help in what to do. Without competent medical attention, the man would die. It was a minor miracle the marshal had recovered so well.

The host had promised immortality, but his coffins didn't work, and there were three more men still alive inside them who might be suffocating.

He started to open the T-bolts on one of the coffins. Dawn joined him and helped and together they opened the tank, working quickly and ignoring the liquid draining around their feet. The man inside was unconscious but breathing. They dragged him to a space on the floor of the operating room. Dawn found a bundle of vacuum-packed towels and dried him off. Tremors ran through his body. They got the next two out. They were in no better shape.

"They all need a hospital," she said.

Miles wiped his hands on a towel. "Watch them. Keep them warm. I'll try to get to the surface. Lock the door behind me."

"If you don't come back, I'll have to come looking."

He couldn't tell if she was joking. "I wouldn't expect otherwise."

There was nothing left to say as he eased the latch open and cracked the vault door. The large bot they had disabled was now parked to one side of the widest section of corridor. A second machine of similar build stood next to it. It had a red eye which stared at them. But the drone didn't move as he stuck his head out and scanned the blacked-out cul-de-sac. It was empty.

Dawn handed him a large glowstick from a first aid locker. The feeble green light barely cut the gloom. He was an easy target for any lurking drones out there waiting for him.

Miles took a tentative step towards the new bot. It actually *looked* new, with yellow plastic panels with nary a scratch. He waved the stick in front of the eye. Touched the cool surface, and one of its limbs planted firmly onto the floor. As he rounded the machine, he saw he'd need tools to get to the power plant to disable it, and Insight reminded him of this particular model's theft deterrence that might be activated if he pressed his luck.

He gave Dawn a wave. She pushed the door closed and, with a final click of the latch, he was alone. His breathing sounded like bellows as he walked up the slope of the shaft.

Lights were coming his way.

The smooth corridor had no place to hide. His laser made a poor hand weapon, and all the bots had to do was keep their distance and burn him down. But then came voices. Three, no, four. Men. Women. If they were Metal Heads coming to save their master, he could only hope they wouldn't recognize him.

Bright white beams cut into the gloom and would find him in moments.

He put the burner away and called out, "Hello up there."

The voices stopped talking. Several shadows wearing headlamps. A flashlight caught him in the face.

"Who are you?" a woman asked.

"I sent the S.O.S."

They whispered among themselves.

After a moment, the woman stepped closer. "This your mine?"

"If you get that light out of my face, we can talk—"

"Hands where I can see them."

A young man with straw-colored hair and an earpiece came forward and patted him down. Found the burner. Took his glowstick.

"Where's the rest of your gang?" the woman asked.

"I'm not a Metal Head. I'm a passenger on the Seraph Express. The train was ambushed and robbed."

"And what are you doing down here?"

"It's a long story. I've got people who need medical attention. Do you have a radio?"

***

Two of the strangers escorted him out of the mine and up the ladder. At the top of the fake well, they were met with more people, all in work clothes and all armed. The woman and one of her group hadn't come with them. Every time Miles protested to get them to return to the vault, he got a shove and finally a threat.

"So much as twitch that trick arm of yours, you'll be sorry," the blond man said.

He was left to ponder if his treatment was because of the Metal Head's reputation or if they had reason to fear cyborgs in general. But he kept quiet and could only hope these rescuers were there to help. Three desert runners were parked around the well. The shed had been demolished but still stood on one upright wall. The delivery dog was gone.

Now that they were out of the mine, a blue glow on the horizon signaled the coming of dawn. Several lanterns illuminated the faces of the rescuers. Hard, sun-beaten, lean. They were picking through the camp and packing tools and stripped machine parts into the trailer of one of the runners.

Scavengers or opportunists, he decided.

"Take what you want," Miles said. "No one alive down there is going to argue. I think the mine operators are all dead."

The blond man licked his teeth. "Tried robbing them and tripped on their security, did you?"

"Not a robber. We have a Seraph marshal with us. I'm asking you to call anyone with Herron-Cauley and let them know what happened with the train. Call Seraph too. I'm sure you'll get a reward."

"Doubt it. Just stay put until Eleanor comes back up."

The blond man busied himself with a tablet without touching the screen. Miles recognized a wireless interface when he saw one. While the man had no visible enhancements, he was a cyborg, which meant the scavengers didn't belong to any of the Luddite cliques. And in the blond's case, the tech was invisible and probably expensive.

One man had climbed a ladder propped up against a leaning antenna tower, which Miles had missed. He was cutting a wire with a pair of pliers. If that was how their SOS got out, their message was now interrupted. A second scavenger lingered nearby, a carbine cradled in his arms.

"Can I get some water?" Miles asked.

The blond blinked hard, and the screen went dark. "Once we have all of you together, we'll care for your every need."

Carbine man's eyes were shifting between Miles and the blond. He was rocking back and forth ever so slightly. Nerves. Miles knew the look. While the man might have been strung out, Miles understood that untrained people about to do violence got shaky. It did something to their voice, their eyes. They lost their composure and the ability to keep their hands steady. Even trained soldiers experienced it. There was little an enhancement could do to completely override the natural dumping of adrenaline into the bloodstream. It was the primal brain entering fight or flight, and these boys didn't look like they were about to run.

"Is that your boss down the ladder?" Miles asked. "Eleanor? If you have a comm line to her, I'd love to chat."

The blond tucked the tablet away. "Time for that later."

"I think this is the perfect time. She's sitting on a treasure chest of tech here. We have no claim to it. You let us walk, we leave."

"Just shut up."

"Sure. Fine. But it's going to get complicated for you and yours real soon. We put our message out to everyone in Seraph, and not just over the radio. That means more marshals, maybe the militia, and whatever posse they collect."

"We'll be out of here in no time."

Miles kept his voice calm, de-escalation 101. "Good. Leave. No one here is interested in stopping you from whatever it is you're into. And you don't want a heap of trouble following you from here. That means letting us go."

"Wouldn't have it any other way."

But the blond nodded at the carbine man.

A rock near Miles' feet was his only weapon. He went for it. Threw. The carbine man blurted something as he deflected the stone with his firearm. But the blond was quick, drawing, aiming, firing. Miles dove and tumbled and felt a hot sting graze his thigh. He hit the ground near the mouth of the well, then elbow-crawled away. The blond stepped over a pile of debris and came for him.

With no cover, Miles rolled onto his back and showed his palms. The blond raised his weapon.

A brilliant spotlight turned the early morning gloom into day. A buzzing drone hovered over them. From up the canyon came the sound of whining engines. Several multi-wheeled vehicles with headlights blazing rolled towards them.

The blond holstered his weapon and motioned for carbine man to do the same. A squad of troopers dressed head to toe in beige plastic armor deployed. Everyone raised their hands.

Miles did too.

Chapter Twenty-Four

The HC emblazoned on the armored guard's shoulder plate told Miles what he needed to know.

Herron-Cauley, the corporation which owned the train and rail line, was here.

They proceeded to line everyone up and get them seated cross-legged in the dirt with their hands on their heads. Miles tried to stay on the opposite side of the lineup from carbine man in case the twitchy salvager tried anything, but one of the HC security team ordered Miles down next to him.

"This one's bleeding," a guard said.

Soon an unarmored man in a beige and white jumpsuit and carrying a small duffle bag tended to Miles' leg. The medic slapped a disinfectant pad onto the thigh wound.

Miles winced. "There's more down that ladder who need help. Three miners who had been trapped in hibernation pods. The train engineer. One of your people, a lawyer, Dawn Moriti, and Marshal Barma."

The medic didn't appear interested.

One of the armored goons raised her visor. "And who are you?"

"Just someone trying to get to Seraph."

She spoke, but the guttural sounds spoken into the throat microphone weren't meant for anyone not on the Herron-Cauley goon squad com network. She had pips on her collar, but Miles couldn't get a count to know what rank she held in the corporation's private security force. The armored squad grouped up and descended the ladder. More HC personnel emerged from the vehicles. One man sat atop a turret and swept a heavy weapon around, aiming at the lip of the canyon above them.

"*Bryer Actual 203 flechette support rifle,*" Insight said. "*Anti-machine, anti-material, anti-personnel. Air-cooled. Capable of 1,100 rounds per minute.*"

Miles didn't shut Insight up this time as it yammered on while the medic finished with the last of the dressing and let him pull up his pants.

"What's the news on the train?" Miles asked.

The medic put his supplies away. "Two dead. Several injured. If you're really a passenger, then you'll be taken care of."

130

And what if he wasn't? But Miles decided it was best to wait and see what the morning would bring. He felt a surge of relief. The host hadn't gotten his attack off the ground. Whether Miles had stopped it by pulling the plug on the host or if some other obstacle had prevented the assault, who knew?

When Dawn emerged from the well along with the Herron-Cauley officer, she accepted help to climb out. Her burned arm had medical foam coating it. She consulted with the officer for a moment before approaching Miles.

"Can I get up now?" he asked.

She helped him rise.

He was grateful for the numbing tingle masking the pain of his thigh wound as he dusted his pants off. "Where's the marshal?"

"They're bringing him now. What happened up here?"

"Just scavengers. They heard your message and got here first. Cut them loose. We have enough problems to clear up."

She said, "We'll consider it. That's not my concern right now. You are."

The medic placed Dawn's injured arm in a sling. Dawn's good hand kept touching the pocket of her purple jacket. No bulge, so it wasn't her pistol. Something small. When she caught Miles looking, she dropped her hand to her side.

"What about the train?" he asked.

"That's where my people came from and how they got here so fast once they picked up our message."

She motioned for him to join her. He was stiff as they walked away from the others and over to the small mountain of tailings piled high against the wall of red stone.

"You didn't run when you could have," she said.

"After bumping into these folks, I didn't have much of a choice."

"Not just now. You could have taken me out down there before any message went out. Or right after. Why didn't you?"

Miles wasn't sure what kind of answer she was looking for. "Seeing this through seemed like a good idea at the time. And I said I wouldn't run."

"So you're coming back to River City with me."

"You're the one with the private army."

She studied him. Her deep brown eyes revealed nothing about what she might be thinking. Sweat had formed streaks in the coating of dirt on her face.

Voices rose from down the well. Miles went to assist the marshal as he ascended the ladder one rung at a time and paused to rest before finishing the climb.

He nodded his thanks before loosening Miles' grip.

The marshal grumbled, "I hate cyborgs."

"Yeah," Miles said. "I do too."

He limped towards an overturned crate. "I'm going to sit down for a spell. Let me know when we get to return to the train."

One of the security people brought Barma a blanket and gave him a water bottle. Miles found a spot next to him.

The sun rose. The temperature began to climb, promising another hot day.

After what felt like an hour of everyone milling about with little happening and more of the HC people descending the ladder, the engineer was brought up, strapped to a stretcher. He had a breathing mask in place over his mouth and nose and a palm-sized medical monitor attached to an exposed bicep. The medic supervised the extraction as the engineer was taken to one of the vehicles marked with a red cross. Dawn joined them. Then she climbed in, and the ambulance did a three-point turn and drove off.

The marshal pulled the blanket over his shoulder tight. "Huh. Guess we don't rate."

The security team brought the three miners up next. These likewise were taken to a vehicle which lingered for a while before heading off.

Miles could only guess what Dawn's departure meant. An expression of confidence that he wouldn't try to flee? Or had she passed orders down to the security grunts, and they'd take it from there and haul Miles back to Meridian?

But even as the salvage gang was kept under guard, he and the marshal didn't have anyone watching over them. A while later, another Herron-Cauley vehicle rolled up. A pair of medics assisted the marshal into the vehicle, and Miles went with them.

Chapter Twenty-Five

The Herron-Cauley driver was on the radio. "Confirmed, Marshal Barma is with me. We're heading for Wood Creek. ETA two-and-a-half hours. Confirm route clearance, please."

Miles couldn't hear the response, as the driver wore a headset. Wood Creek Hospital, according to Insight, was in Seraph. What would be waiting for him there? He tried to clear the fog from his brain, but exhaustion and the hum of the engine kept lulling him to sleep.

"Take me to the train," the marshal said.

"Sorry, sir, we have orders to get you to a medical facility. The train passengers are being assisted, and you need a doctor."

"This isn't a request. You get me to that train, or I'm taking that steering wheel away from you."

Neither the driver nor the two medics appeared willing to test whether the marshal was capable. The driver informed his network of the change of destination. They took a turn, which bounced them over broken ground and up a rise thick with gnarled trees growing among the sandstone.

A family of quail trotted out in front of them, barely missing getting run over. It was the first wildlife Miles had seen. While River City had parks and bio-reserves, much of the wilds beyond the habitable zone were wastelands with no animal life. The desert still had some of its native flora and fauna.

The marshal gripped a handle fixed above the door. His jaw was tight, and he winced with every jarring bump. "Any objections to not going straight to Seraph?"

It took Miles a moment to realize the marshal was talking to him. "Be good to see that the passengers are getting cared for."

"Is that your deal? Looking after people? Coming to save me wasn't smart."

"Maybe it wasn't. And I don't have a deal. I was just trying to get from point A to point B when someone broke our train."

"Something which you know nothing about."

Miles was too tired to argue. "I'm not a Metal Head."

"Probably not. But I don't think that host is, either. I can't figure out his angle. He was playing the gang. If you learned anything while I was stuck in that tube, somehow I'm guessing you're not going to share. Maybe it doesn't matter. Don't think I didn't hear you and Dawn whispering. What does she have on you? Or what do you have on her?"

"Nothing which would concern a Seraph marshal."

"Huh. Maybe we're both best off minding our business."

After a final series of jolts, the driver got them on a relatively smooth road. Miles was suddenly not tired as the train came into view. A pair of buses and several service vehicles were parked around the train. Armed sentries stood on the rail bed, and a drone circled in wide arcs over the surrounding area. Risky using a flying machine, but there were enough clouds that anyone watching up in low orbit might miss it.

The bedraggled train passengers were queuing up to board the buses.

The marshal leaned forward to the driver and pointed. "Pull up there."

He didn't wait for the vehicle to roll to a complete stop before piling out. Miles slid out and caught up with him. The marshal made a beeline for Paxton Walker, his prisoner. The cuffs were off. Paxton stiffened as the marshal took him by the elbow.

Paxton said, "Why Marshal Barma, I see you've survived your exploits, as did our deadeye friend."

"Sorry to disappoint you," the marshal said. "I've got a ride for us."

Paxton's head sank as the marshal marched him back to the HC runner. Miles watched them leave and took his place in the back of the line for one of the buses.

The woman ahead of him was Mrs. Fish, the owner of the expensive furniture lost in the drone strike. "The marshal procured *private* transportation?"

"Seems so. Maybe if you hurry, you can hitch a ride."

The runner wasn't waiting and left a cloud of dust behind it as it took the marshal and his prisoner away.

Chapter Twenty-Six

Mrs. Fish sat next to Miles, her butt on the edge of the seat as if she didn't want to sit back against the faux fabric material. The bus wasn't clean, Miles had to admit, but there was cool air blowing, and one of the train people handed out packets of granola and bottles of water. She also studiously avoided the shared armrest where Miles was leaning.

He guessed he was a sight, plentifully bestrewn with all the grime the desert could throw at him, along with blood, sweat, and hibernation tank preserving fluid.

When the bus hit its first bump, Mrs. Fish was almost thrown out of her seat. Miles caught her and planted her down. She grabbed both arm rests and nodded her thanks before breathing through a lacy handkerchief.

Miles took in the final sight of the train through the window before allowing himself to drift off.

Metal Heads. An army of spider bots. A half-dead maniac with a ripper addiction. A bounty hunter looking to repo Miles' jailbroken implants. Yet something else gnawed at the edge of his thoughts.

The robbery and aerial strike.

There had been a spider with a laser targeting system which had directed the drone bomb into the passenger car. A waste of ordinance? Or overkill on the part of the gang and a warning to not come after them?

Crazy people did crazy things. How many perfectly good getaways had been spoiled because the perp needed to stop for a meal, a bathroom break, or a booty call? Miles had once busted a pair of female thieves who had robbed the safe of a card room in the back of one of the bars on his army base. They had stolen the owner's motorcycle and could have made a clean break, as it had been a busy night for the MPs. But instead of fleeing into River City, the brain donors had stopped at one of their boyfriends to confront him about his cheating with another woman. Shots fired had brought the entire force down on them.

If the host was responsible, then why had he been so direct in his abduction of the engineer after the drone strike?

The V and Y mine where the host resided had charging ports for delivery dogs. Yet they had all been empty until the dog he and the marshal had followed arrived. The Metal Head cave didn't have a charge depot, and the village of The Place Where We Sang the Night Hymnal only had one.

Unrelated details, surely, and nothing which should have concerned him. The marshal had his man. The Metal Heads were no doubt scattering in the face of so many Herron-Cauley security troopers swarming the area. The host was dead. His living tomb held no treasures stolen from the train except for the engineer and the marshal.

But the delivery dogs were all over the desert. Someone had pinched something and had gotten away with it.

He was trying to make the clues fit the thin theory formulating in the back of his mind. A rookie mistake. Work the evidence. Your gut and what you want the crime to be had no place in good police work. And it wasn't his job, he kept reminding himself.

The Metal Heads were robbers. The host had plainly stated what he wanted from the people he abducted. Whatever else had been stolen from the train just hadn't been discovered.

It was always simple. Except when it wasn't.

Thinking about it all felt as if he were juggling a dozen objects of differing sizes and shapes, some round, some sharp, and some on fire. His arrival in Seraph meant he could let them all drop into the sand and fall away behind him as he finished what he set out to do.

Contact the surgeon. Make a new appointment. Lay the groundwork for peace between him and Dillan and find peace.

***

They were passing through a greenhouse district. This went on and on, the bus whisking past hundreds of glass structures, some industrial-sized and others merely covered plant beds and private gardens. Homes rose among the desert farms, a variety of eclectic domes, huts, and houses as varied as the crops. Seraph had become a haven for the farmers who wanted to experiment with non-approved variants of grains, vegetables, and fruits, be they unadulterated or genetically altered to the point of being unrecognizable to any farmer who had worked the soil in generations past.

Lawbreakers, according to Meridian.

Miles felt he was in good company. Yet as he entertained the notion he might slip off the bus and away to find a replacement device so he could make the phone call, the bus slowed. They approached a line of armored security in front of a two-floor building of concrete covered in creeper vines and solar panels.

If they were waiting for him, he wasn't going to fight.

Dawn Moriti had made good on her end of the deal. He wouldn't run. But as he followed Mrs. Fish and the rest of the passengers off the bus, he realized the security people weren't Herron-Cauley. No HC logo, for starters. The cops were dressed in desert-speckled helmets and chest pieces which matched the smaller electric cruisers, which were parked everywhere. White lights strobed on the light bars of the vehicles. A milling crowd waited beyond.

When a vehicle departed the building's roundabout, a sign which had been obstructed came into view. Wood Creek Hospital.

Each person off the bus was directed towards the entrance by hospital staff.

An orderly assisted Mrs. Fish, who swooned as soon as the man took her by the arm. Another staff member brought a wheelchair, and she was carted off ahead of the line.

Past the nearest vehicles was the Herron-Cauley ambulance, which had carried Dawn and the chief engineer. At the head of the line were nurses taking people's names as they were admitted. Overseeing it was a tall woman in a blue double-breasted suit and a beehive hairdo. Next to her stood a bald man with an augmentation worn over his eyes and nose. They were carrying on a soft conversation. The woman maintained a terse smile as she nodded greetings to each new patient.

Miles cut past the queue and approached them. "I'm looking for Dawn Moriti."

The woman's mask of pleasant concern never wavered. "Your needs will be cared for once we get everyone checked out."

"I don't need a doctor. Dawn Moriti must have gotten here an hour ago. I have questions about what happened."

"Yes, we all do. Mr. Mendel here is with the rail line and will take your statement and your contact information so you can be compensated for damages."

Mr. Mendel's face appeared pale and waxy. His artificial eyes looked like goggles with concave lenses. One orb fixed on Miles, even as the other continued to watch the line of passengers.

He said, "Your concerns will be attended to once our legal team arrives. Your redress will be generous, Mr...."

"I'm not interested in a ticket refund. Your employee Dawn Moriti is inside the hospital. Tell me where she is, and I'll go talk to her."

He blinked hard. Data streamed across one eye. "Herron-Cauley has no employee by that name."

"You must be looking in the wrong database," Miles said. "She's one of your lawyers. She was brought here with the train's chief engineer and a couple of your medics. She was a passenger in the same car as me."

Both eyes fixed on him. "The chief engineer was indeed brought here. Both medics accompanied him to intensive care where he is being treated. There was no one else with them."

"There was also a driver. He'll tell you. Where is he?"

"The driver, according to the tracker, is at the picnic area on the north side of the hospital grounds and, judging by his elevated heart rate, smoking a stimulant stick. If I may say so, you appear to have suffered a wound. Herron-Cauley is covering all medical expenses. Allow me to take you inside so you can—sir?"

Miles left the corporate front man and the hospital admin and went to find the ambulance driver.

The driver turned off his stim stick and tucked it into a vest pocket as Miles approached. The smell of strawberries and cream wafted about in a swirl of dissipating vapor. The man's green eyes were bloodshot and baggy, and his jumpsuit was stained. His device sat on the picnic table next to him playing electronic violin music. He was nodding along to it.

"Long shift?" Miles asked.

"One of the longest. Crazy night. You were down in that mine, weren't you?"

"Yeah. I was with Dawn Moriti. Seems your corporate spokesman doesn't know her. But you brought her here along with the engineer and the medical team."

The driver's eyes narrowed. "What of it?"

"Where did she go?"

"After the engineer was brought inside by the hospital's crash team, she took off."

She had made it to Seraph, Miles thought. So why had the Herron-Cauley man denied she existed? "Did she say anything to you on your trip?"

"Uh-uh. I was minding the road. So if she had a conversation, it was with the medics. She didn't say anything to them either after our little stop."

Miles leaned closer. "What stop?"

"A few kilometers south of the train. Picked up a box. Weird, but it sounded like stuff got dropped everywhere by those bandits. I would have felt better getting an escort. With Metal Heads roaming the wastes, it's not safe. At least we're getting hazard pay for this rescue op. I'm going back out there once my mandatory break is over and the medics return."

Go back out there.

Would the driver even be able to find the exact spot where Dawn had them stop? The box she had recovered could have been anything. But the evidence was speaking, and he had to listen. The Metal Heads hadn't dropped anything. One of the spider drones had, or a delivery dog, and not by accident.

It begged the question of why Dawn had agreed to go with Miles to help rescue the marshal. Maybe she cared. She had risked her life going down into the mine. But the explosion which had destroyed the freight car could have killed dozens of people. And was the robbery and the host all part of her attempt to steal a single parcel? Or had she somehow learned what the parcel was during her time in the mine with the host's computer? Something more valuable than whatever bounty she would earn bringing him back to Meridian?

At the mine, she had something tucked away in her pocket before departing with the medics. And he hadn't watched her that closely when she was ostensibly working on the host's computer.

"Are you okay?" the driver asked.

Miles didn't answer. The marshal needed to know about Dawn. But she was only one piece of the train puzzle. The fresh tailings, the functioning mining machines at the V, Y, and Company mine which had been in operation after the host had taken it over, and the delivery dogs. The host wasn't just living in the mine, he was running it.

He picked up the driver's device and held it out. "Your thumb?"

The driver didn't argue and unlocked the phone.

Miles turned off the music and spoke into the device. "Seraph Marshal's office. Marshal Barma."

The marshal had lost his phone during the robbery, but hopefully his office would have a line on him. A chime dinged.

A pleasant-sounding woman who Insight identified as an AI said, "Please state your name and the reason for your call. If this is an emergency, hang up and tell the Seraph network 'Emergency.'"

As the message began to repeat in Chinese, he said, "Miles Kim. The train crimes. Barma, pick up."

When the marshal answered, he sounded distant and echoey. "What do you want?"

"Do I need to wait for you to finish up and wash your hands?"

"I'm not in the can. I'm at my desk. I've got my prisoner checked in and an egg sandwich in front of me, and then I'm going home and getting some sleep. How can I help you?"

"Dawn Moriti has gone missing. Not like abducted missing, but she vanished. She's not Herron-Cauley, or at least not who she said she was. Whatever box was taken from the train, she picked it up before coming to Seraph."

After some shuffling, the marshal's voice sounded louder. "Go on."

"I'm thinking she was either Plan B for the robbery, or she intercepted what was stolen from the train."

"That's a lot of speculation. This isn't Seraph business. Check with Herron-Cauley. They've got security all over the place out in that desert. So why are you calling *me* with this?"

"Because you're the only law man I know in Seraph, and you care," Miles said. "Plus there's a Seraph angle. You mentioned the delivery dogs are run by a business consortium. I think Dawn took the memory chips from the host's computer to cover her tracks. During our time down in the vault after the host was disconnected, she had the opportunity to send a message to one of the dogs to redirect the package and drop it off where only she could recover it. If the dogs are run by a Seraph company, it puts this in your jurisdiction, doesn't it?"

"Yeah, it does. But it only leads to more questions. What was stolen? I'm guessing the train company won't share, so unless the owner comes forward to me with a complaint, we won't know."

"Whatever it is, it's valuable. More than any bounty on me. She was going to take me back to Meridian to collect on jailbroken implants."

The marshal took a moment to blow his nose. "This place is going to kill me. You know telling me this isn't smart, right? I work my share of bounties. It pays for my lavish lifestyle choices."

"If you want to grab me and bring me back to River City, so be it. But people died over this train robbery."

"Hmm. So let's say Dawn Moriti figured out how to grab the loot. She's in the wind, and, according to you, she has the memory chips from the host's terminal. That's your smoking gun."

Miles took a few steps away from the listening driver. "I'm sure she'll ditch those quickly. You need to figure out who is on the receiving end of this. There has to be a buyer. The host wasn't working alone and was only a middleman. Think about everything we saw: a functioning mine on automation, sorters, digging machines, and miners who had been brain-ripped so the host could access their skills. According to the notebook I found in the miner's village, the V, Y, and Company mine might have been claim jumped by the host or the Metal Heads as long as a year ago. But we found fresh medical supplies. The host was sending off ore and making purchases. I'm guessing ultimately from Seraph."

"You're guessing again."

"That's where the evidence keeps leading."

The ambulance driver was finished with his vape but appeared too nervous to ask for his device back. Meanwhile, the line into the hospital was mostly processed. The Seraph militia was busy talking among themselves, and no one paid him any attention.

"This sounds like a can of worms," the marshal said. "A lot of important people have their fingers in the transportation and delivery business. I'll have to get warrants. Do things carefully and by the book."

"It's your town. I'm leaving it in your hands."

"You and I are the only eyewitnesses. How do I reach you?"

Miles hesitated before he answered. *You can't reach me. You won't reach me. I'll be...what? Lying on a surgery table and counting down from a hundred for the last time?*

"I'll check in with you tomorrow." Miles ended the call and handed the device over to the ambulance driver.

That concluded Miles' obligation. He had his own appointment to make. Would need a phone. Before that, a few hours of sleep so he could digest the events of the past couple of days and try to know if he had just lied to the marshal.

Crossing the hospital lot, he headed for the street.

Miles was cutting through the small crowd who were gawking from beyond a row of barriers. A hospital security guard was keeping the spectators away from the hospital.

A voice from behind him called out.

"Dad?"

Chapter Twenty-Seven

His son, Dillan, approached through the crowd. Taller than he remembered, broader in shoulder, with a patch of fuzz on his chin that would never fill out. He was dressed in a dark green kurta, the long garment and slacks airy in the heat, with his feet clad in black sandals.

"What are you doing here?" Miles blurted.

"I heard what happened to the train. Some lady left a message you were on board. So I came to see after not being able to reach you."

"I left my phone on the base." *So as not to be tracked*, but he left that part out.

When his son embraced him, it took Miles a second to respond in kind. But then he didn't want to let go. It was Dillan who broke off the hug and gave his father an appraising look.

"I'm a mess," Miles said. "I wanted to go clean up. But look at you. You're dressing like you belong here."

"I live in Seraph."

"Yeah, I know. Look, Dillan, I didn't mean to surprise you. I tried to call before getting on the train. I tried to call for months. Every time I picked up the phone, I wimped out."

"I probably wouldn't have answered, dad. I'm sorry to say that, but it's the truth. But you haven't answered me. Why *are* you here?"

"I wanted to make sure you were okay. See it with my own eyes."

Dillan spread his hands. "Haven't starved to death playing music, if that was what you were worrying about."

Miles' comment had slipped out on one of the last nights when Seo Yeun, Dillan's mother, was still alive. Dillan had just revealed his plans to go to Seraph with a couple of friends from school, along with a girl whom he had been dating for two months and was now his "soulmate." They all played in a band together. "And do what?" Miles had asked. "Play in bars and street corners for handouts?" He had never made it to any of Dillan's performances. Didn't get it, hadn't wanted to get how all that noise equated to a sound anyone would call music. And even if it were art, how would it pay rent?

It hadn't been a fight, not really, not like the times Dillan and Miles ended their exchanges with a slammed door and silent treatments which would last a week. Only Seo Yeun could get them talking to each other again.

Then Seo Yeun died, and they had no one to broker peace.

Dillan had left days after her body had been buried in the conservation park where it would biodegrade. Miles planted a myrtle tree above the spot the following week. Then he went back to work.

"I just needed to make sure..." Miles began. Hesitated.

...you aren't wasting your life.

...you aren't homeless and strung out on shabu or a sim junkie.

...you aren't lost.

"I had to set eyes on you and see you. That's all."

Dillan's jaw grew tight. "I'm working. Erin and I broke up, but I'm seeing someone new. I finished my degree in art therapy this past winter, and I'm seeing my first patients. It's kids, mostly. And yes, it pays."

"You're helping people," Miles said.

"I hope I am. Not what I expected to be doing. But I play nights and weekends with a new group. We do ambient new-earth house, some late dream trance, a little old school electrogrind."

"I don't know what any of that is."

"You would if you ever came to one of my gigs."

"I'm here now. Is that an invitation?"

"I don't know. Dad, I don't know what you're expecting from me. I don't know if I'm ready to have you in my life. And you just showing up..."

"I'm not here to upset you. Can we go somewhere and sit? It's been a long night."

Dillan said, "You're hurt. I saw you limping. What happened on the train? And why aren't you checking into the hospital?"

Miles looked back as the last of his bus group was entering the emergency room. "I liberated my implants before leaving River City. It means they're stolen."

"Why would you do that?"

"Because I've earned them. They decided there was no way they could remove them without killing me. It meant I would have to live there until I die so they could reclaim the parts of me which belong to them."

"Why didn't you tell me you were going to do this? I would have come. I would have helped."

"Then you'd be on Meridian's wanted list, too. The woman who called you is a bounty hunter. What did she say exactly?"

"That you were on the train that was attacked, and that I should go and see you. That's it. Didn't leave a name. The call came from an anonymous number."

Miles scanned the crowd of gawkers. No familiar faces. No one paying him or Dillan any attention. Why had Dawn Moriti found and called Dillan? Surely she could get the Seraph cops to scoop Miles up so she could take him into custody. A power move? *I can get to you when I want to.* Or was it a gesture of peace, a professional nod after what they had been through? Whatever she had recovered in the desert was worth more than some out-of-date hardware on an old lawman and the bounty it would bring.

Everything he could come up with were only guesses, and he was tired. But the not knowing was a lit fuse in his mind, which he forced himself to ignore.

For the moment.

"Dad?"

"I'm not going to the hospital. I got patched up already. Now I just want to sit down with you and have you tell me everything about what you do and who you are."

Epilogue

The reunion with Dillan didn't go as planned. A series of messages kept distracting his son, and less than ten minutes into their sitting down, Dillan left. An emergency with one of his clients.

"How about this evening?" Miles had almost asked, "Or breakfast tomorrow? I'll be here."

But Miles had only said goodbye and watched Dillan hurry off down the sidewalk away from the tea shop where they had taken one of the outside tables. A trellis covered in wisteria shaded him from the rising sun. The earlier clouds had vanished. They had ordered nothing. Miles got up and pushed both chairs in before walking out to the sidewalk and considering where he would go.

He returned to the hospital. The Herron-Cauley executive was seated just inside the door. One of the cyborg's eyes watched Miles approach before the man tore his attention away from a tablet.

Miles did his best to flash a warm smile. "Remember me? You mentioned something about a refund. I'm here to cash in."

***

He had enough for a pleasant room in an excellent hotel for a few weeks, maybe longer if he was careful with the credits he had received. Generous, as far as compensation for a ticket, but far short of anything which would serve as compensation for the night he had experienced. How much would Mrs. Fish extract from the company, he wondered?

Not his concern.

The nearby hotel was missing its front door but didn't ask for his ID if he was willing to pay a higher rate. He paid. After trudging up to the second floor and finding his room, he remembered little after washing up and his head hitting the pillow.

By the time he stirred, the sun had set. His head pounded. After drinking a couple of glasses of water in the bathroom, he examined his reflection. Nothing new there. He pushed aside the blackout drapes and gazed outside at the orange streetlights illuminating the avenue below. Light foot and vehicle traffic passed by in either direction. Compared to River City, Seraph was dark at night and quiet.

He didn't want to think about anything. Needed more sleep. An argument in the neighboring room had given way to soft groans and thumping, which he tuned out. He would have returned to bed but for the nagging thought which crystalized, and it had nothing to do with Dillan or the surgeon or whether he would ever consider returning to Meridian.

He had missed something.

Someone.

Mr. Zoon's daughter Hill. She was still out there.

He got dressed and went downstairs to the small lobby, which was little more than the check-in desk and a cramped alcove and couch where guests could wait for a ride and not be out in the weather.

A sign propped up on the reception desk read No Vacancy. The smell of cooking cabbage permeated, and the muffled voices of a serial played from beyond a curtain behind the desk. Miles looked for a buzzer or bell or call box but found nothing. He wrapped with his metal knuckles on the wood.

Miles flinched when an unseen speaker crackled. "No refunds after check-in," a sharp voice snapped.

"The accommodations are everything I could hope for. The bed's soft, the water's softer, and the soundproofing lets in all the ambience of the surrounding rooms."

The voice let out a long sigh. "What do you want?"

"A phone. Or a place to buy one."

"Data kiosk by Wood Creek Hospital. If you have the credits, grab a device from the drugstore on Gallina Road."

"You are the epitome of the gracious host. Thank you."

A click, and the speaker went silent. Miles headed out and looked up at the misting rain which sprinkled down in soft sheets. Along the avenue, patterns of trickling droplets marked trails down the clinging soil caked on the parked vehicles.

The drug store had its closed sign turned up but the lights were on. Through the glass door, a bleary-eyed clerk in a green apron was checking a customer.

Miles pushed open the door, and a buzzer chimed.

"We're closed," the clerk announced without looking up from the order she was scanning.

Miles ignored her, heading down the aisles until he found the electronics. He grabbed a device, scanned the label, and confirmed it would work on the Seraph network. The price was five times higher than a similar device purchased in River City.

The checker's jaw was tight when she scanned the phone and waited for payment. She didn't make eye contact.

"For what it's worth, it's for a good cause," Miles said. "Long shift?"

She gave a humorless laugh. "Aren't they all?"

The clerk locked the door after he left.

Miles signed the phone into the network. Called the marshal's office. If Barma was in, he wasn't picking up. Miles left a message. Hung up. Considered the options of calling Herron-Cauley or the militia.

Walking to an overhang near the tea shop, he searched for vehicle rentals. The front page on each service told him what he feared he'd find. They required a deposit. His compensation credits wouldn't cover it. He needed another plan. He next searched for guides, independent surveyors, and drivers. None would book anything which would leave that evening. So he made an appointment for 5 a.m. the next morning and went back to his room.

***

The surveyor met him in front of a materials yard a few blocks away. His ride was a six-wheel narrow-body runner, the back half full of equipment and tools. To the east, the sky was turning lighter shades of blue. The man gave Miles a once-over before double checking his device.

"Says 'undisclosed location' is our destination. Before we go anywhere, it's time to disclose."

"The Place Where We Sang the Night Hymnal," Miles said.

"Never heard of it."

"Two hundred six kilometers north-northeast."

The surveyor entered the information. "Full-day trip, then. But I get back in by sundown. That's the deal. So travel both ways cuts into how much time we spend on the ground—wait a sec. Area's got a security flag. Herron-Cauley has forty miles on either side of their new track on lockdown. Says no one in or out."

"They don't own the desert."

"That may be true, but out there they might as well be masters of all they survey with the amount of guns they carry. Even the Red Banner militia gets out of their way. I'm sorry, mister, but this is too hot."

The surveyor was checking the cargo straps on his vehicle's load.

Miles said, "This isn't a mining expedition. I just need someone who knows the area who can do the driving. We're going out to save someone. It's a young girl who got left out in the desert."

"This has something to do with the train heist, doesn't it? Maybe some other prospector or driver might want to play looky-loo with you, not me."

"If it's Herron-Cauley you're worried about, we can call the militia. They could give us permission so we can make the trip. You won't even have to get out of your vehicle. And I'm offering you a bump to our agreed-upon rate."

Using his device, Miles loaded a credit chip.

The surveyor checked the amount. "That's...incredibly generous. But you're not selling it. Look, I'm not heartless. If what you say is true, tell the militia. Tell Herron-Cauley. Have them go searching for this girl. But I don't want to risk violating an HC security warning. Some of those boys shoot first and don't bother with the questions. Or they might seize my runner. That puts me out of work, and your credits won't come close to covering my end if that happens."

Miles stood helplessly by as the surveyor climbed in his vehicle and departed. Perhaps the man was right. The train company security might find Hill. But there was also the likelihood that they were sweeping the desert and going after anyone who might be associated with the Metal Heads, would find the cave near The Place Where We Sang the Night Hymnal, and she would get swept away with whatever violence would follow.

He didn't feel sanguine about contacting the militia. If their role stopped at the edge of Seraph city limits, then they'd be no help. He'd have to try other drivers. Surely there was someone who wanted the last of his credits, even if they could get him close to the hideout.

He was on his eighteenth call, getting a runaround from another of the services when he wouldn't disclose the destination and turned down by others when he told them where he wanted to go, when an incoming message pinged.

It was from Marshal Barma. *Call me. Now.*

When Miles tapped the marshal's name, Barma picked up immediately. "Don't robots ever sleep?"

"The older models don't. You got my message? The girl, Hill, she was inside the Metal Head's hideout. I need to go get her out of there. I know you and the militia can't do much outside of Seraph, but someone has to have some kind of authority—"

"They got her."

Miles felt a chilled hand grip his spine. "What?"

"Not like that. I got your message last night. Bully me for waking up and checking my phone. I sent the request up the line. My boss shared it with the duty captain of the Red District militia."

"I saw them outside the hospital. Didn't fill me with confidence."

"Don't think Red District was there. That was the Yellow Tigers. That's the mayor's police force. They're useless. Red District still has some original settlers running their show. They sometimes patrol the desert and do what they can to keep the roads safe for everyone. They sent a runner up to Zoon's little burg and found the cave. The Metal Heads were gone, but they found the girl. She didn't make it easy, from what I hear, but they brought her to Seraph."

"Is she okay?"

"I haven't laid eyes on her. Their patrol officer placed her in a youth home under the care of a psychologist. Good place. They'll figure out if she has any family, take care of her if she doesn't."

"Can I see her?"

The marshal paused. "If I'm there, yeah. They don't know you. Place is secure. We can set something up this afternoon. But I've got paperwork to do first. Most of it thanks to you."

That was it. Hill was safe. Miles wanted to confirm it with his own eyes, but he dared hope it was true.

He'd take the marshal up on the offer to visit with her, even as he doubted Hill would understand where she was and was undoubtedly having a rough day which would only get worse once she realized she could never go back to whatever kind of life she had been living. As broken as the Meridian military and civilian organizations could be, sometimes at the end of the day they would care for their own. Hopefully, Seraph could do the same. And surely his small windfall could help her situation.

He'd only need enough to grab a room for a week or two, a *quiet* one, and to pay for food. The rest could be hers.

"One more thing," the marshal said. "I have a message for you from Beatrix Fish. She was looking for you last night and called a few times."

"What does she want?"

"I'm not your secretary. I'll forward the message. Text me when you want to visit Hill."

The marshal ended the call.

A forwarded voicemail popped up. "Miles Kim. This is Beatrix Fish. You proved most resourceful during our train misadventure. I understand you were a lawman working for Meridian. I'm inquiring if you're for hire? I have an urgent matter I'd like your help with."

The message came with contact information. Miles stared at his phone for a moment. He was nobody in Seraph. And he had his own plans, didn't he? Yet with his son at least willing to entertain the notion they might see one another again, and the welfare of an orphaned girl to check on, he was going to be around for at least a short while.

He called.

I hope you enjoyed The Seraph Engine. Please take a moment to leave a rating or review. Even a short comment can help small-press authors find new readers.

The Atomic Ballerina, book two of the Old Chrome series, continues Miles Kims' adventure.

When Beatrix Fish enlists Miles Kim's help to find her missing daughter Agatha, he discovers the child is more than a simple runaway.

His investigation thrusts him into a web of deceit, where the richest family in Seraph is more interested in protecting secrets than finding Agatha, and someone is willing to do anything to keep Miles from uncovering the truth.

As the case grows more complex with each turn and twist, Miles will need to navigate the upper crust of Seraph high society and its darkest corners to bring the girl home.

Did you love *The Seraph Engine*? Then you should read *Shadows of Mars* by I.O. Adler!

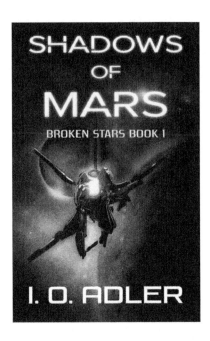

The message from Carmen Vincent's mother wasn't possible. She died in the Mars base disaster two years ago.

But when government agents show up at Carmen's door, she realizes the message is no hoax. Someone is still trying to cover up the disaster and the reason why Earth abandoned its space program.

It's a race to discover the truth of what happened on Mars before Carmen loses her mother for a second time.

I.O. Adler's relentlessly entertaining space opera adventure channels the excitement of The Expanse and the Mass Effect games.